LARK

BOOKS BY SALLY WATSON

Lark
Witch of the Glens
Poor Felicity
To Build a Land
Mistress Malapert
Highland Rebel

LARK

By Sally Watson

HOLT, RINEHART AND WINSTON
NEW YORK · CHICAGO · SAN FRANCISCO

To my loving and lovable sister Marilyn, and to Karin and Debi, who take after their mother.

 Published simultaneously in Canada by Holt, Rinehart and Winston of Canada, Limited/ Library of Congress Catalog Card Number: 64-18258/ Printed in the United States of America/ 99254-0414/ First Edition

Contents

1

The Cottage with the Herb Garden

JAMES

The man in sober Puritan dress paused and glanced behind him, for he thought he had heard a sound that was neither squirrel nor bird. But except for the small rustles and twitterings that belonged there, the forest lay still and shadowy in the long summer twilight. He turned and went on, for he was anxious to see his family, and even the disturbing young niece he was raising at God's request.

Behind him a brown shadow moved slightly and became a wiry youth with a lean brown face which wore an expression of amusement mixed with wariness. The wariness was quite understandable, for in Cromwell's England of 1651 it was not in the least safe to be a messenger for the defeated Royalists. The amusement was simply the love of this exciting game—for James Trelawney had an adventurous spirit as well as a deep loyalty to his young king, Charles II, who had been crowned in Scotland last January, though he could hardly have been said to have ruled yet.

James made a wry face as he went on silently through the forest, moving with almost the lithe grace of a Gypsy—though he was not one. It was his private opinion that the Scots—or at least the Lowland Scots—were all quite mad, and he wished Charles had not associated himself with them, even to be crowned. He had a dark suspicion that no good would come of the alliance, especially now that the Scots had decided to invade England with Charles at their head. That was *not* the way, thought James, to win the love and trust of the English.

But that was not James's affair, thank goodness. He simply served his king in whatever way he could, mainly by delivering messages; a job which became more exciting the further the Scottish army moved into England. But this particular errand pleased him, for he loved old Mistress Tillyard and looked forward to a savory meal and an evening of talk once his messages were delivered.

A mile or so further there was a clearing near the edge of the wood, where an old cottage nestled in the middle of an herb garden. A light flickered through the drawn curtains. James tapped softly.

LARK

Lark set an egg carefully in her basket, kilted her full gray skirts a little higher, and went on searching among the hay with an industry that was truly impressive. A painter (assuming that God and Cromwell had approved such an un-

Puritan occupation) might have done a portrait of the small-boned figure with snowy cap and collar and grave round face. He would doubtless have called it "Industrious Puritan Child," in which case he would have been mistaken on all three counts. For Lark was older than she looked, and her private thoughts were still lamentably worldly, and her great industry was simply because Uncle Jeremiah had just arrived home last night and she was trying (though without much hope) to escape one of his interminable family prayers.

"Elizabeth!" The sound came from the house. Lark wrinkled her nose and burrowed further into the hay, seething with rebellious thoughts. She felt that she hated her aunt and uncle and all her cousins, and in addition she was very much displeased with God, so that it would be quite silly to go and pray to Him. It seemed perfectly clear that He must be on Uncle Jeremiah's side.

Uncle Jeremiah, of course, was perfectly certain of this, and that was one reason why Lark was here today instead of being with her own family, now in exile in France. When Lark was born, her uncle took an immediate fancy to her, and decided that she should marry his oldest son. That was back in the days before religion and politics and the Civil Wars had driven their families apart, and Lark could remember his visits quite well. He always told Lark and Will-of-God that they would marry some day, and everyone took it rather as a joke except Lark, who didn't at all like her big cousin, even then.

But to Uncle Jeremiah it was no joke. It was God's Will. He had said so on that awful day more than two years ago when he had brought his whole troop of Roundhead soldiers to her father's home and stolen Lark right away from her family! He said God had particularly arranged the orders that took his troops right past the Lennox home in the most convenient way possible. Clearly He had not wanted Will-of-God's future wife to be brought up in such an ungodly household, but to be raised in a manner worthy of her husband. And off he had ridden with her, in spite of the perfectly blistering things said to him by Lark's mother and grandparents—her father was away at the time, trying to help save the Royalist cause.

But it had already been too late to help poor beheaded King Charles, and the Royalist cause seemed lost with him. All her father had accomplished was to get himself and his family exiled to France, leaving Lark in Uncle Jeremiah's hands.

It had been a dreadful shock to Lark, the adored youngest child in her own family, accustomed to having her own way within reason. Here there was no quick warmth of affection, no teasing, no spoiling, not even any laughter. Lark had been unbelievably unhappy. And for a long time she simply couldn't believe that Uncle Jeremiah was *not* going to take her back, no matter how unhappy she was. Tears did no good, arguments were silenced, rebellion was punished. Pleading was met by the rejoinder that it was All For her Own Good, and God's Will.

Lark learned to be subtle. She wore a mask of meekness in sheer self-defense. She no longer glared and told them she hated them all. Her carefully played role hadn't got her back home—yet—but it had saved her a good deal of unpleasantness, and it had convinced Uncle Jeremiah that he had tamed her, more or less. He would have been very much astonished to know that she still hated him unrelentingly, and was still perfectly determined to get back to her family, be they at the ends of the earth. And she would have no scruples about how she managed it, either! What with one thing and another, Lark had developed into an incredibly determined person on the inside and a splendid actress on the outside.

"Elizabeth!" She was always Elizabeth here, though no one at home had ever called her anything but Lark. She closed her ears stubbornly. It was Will-of-God's voice, and he was, if anything, even more grim and bossy and humorless than his father. Lark hadn't the least intention of marrying him, but she very much hoped to be back with her family before the unpleasant subject should come to a head. In the meantime, she set herself firmly against growing up—or at least against showing it so that people would notice. With considerable help from nature, she was still managing to look and act about ten. Since Puritans didn't celebrate birthdays, she hoped that her aunt and uncle would somehow forget the passage of time.

"Elizabeth! Didn't you hear us calling? You're delaying prayers, you wicked girl!" Will-of-God stood in the doorway frowning into the gloom of the barn. His new full breeches and boots made him look more hulking than ever, and now that he was going into Cromwell's army, in his father's own company, his airs were simply unbearable. Lark would have loved to defy him outright, but she had learned through long experience that it wasn't worth it. It meant either being punished or being prayed over, and she didn't know which she disliked more.

Instead, she turned deceitfully innocent eyes to her

cousin. "Oh," she said guilelessly, "were you calling, Will-of-God? I was trying to find the speckled hen's nest, so we could have lots of eggs for Uncle Jeremiah."

Will-of-God frowned at her. He sometimes entertained uncomfortable suspicions about what really went on in Elizabeth's head. To be sure, she was merely a female, but it was well known that Satan found females particularly easy to corrupt, since they were even more wicked and stupid by nature than males were.

"You should have known, anyway," he said severely. "You knew Father was home, and he always has extra prayers when he's here. I sometimes wonder, Elizabeth, how long it will take to train you into a suitable wife for me."

Lark was by now expert at hiding her feelings, and if she permitted herself a malevolent glance at him, the dimness of the barn hid it. Still, it was impossible to resist a subtle dig now and then at his revolting complacency.

"Perhaps God just predestined me *not* to become a good Puritan," she murmured innocently.

Will-of-God had no answer to this disconcerting idea, which most unfairly attacked him on his home ground. Instead, he turned and led the way masterfully to the house, his delinquent cousin trailing meekly behind.

She knelt—after not too much of a scolding—between her placid cousin Honour and her stolid cousin Repent, wishing for the thousandth time that the paving tiles of the floor were less hard, or that she had a cushion hidden beneath her long skirts, or that Uncle Jeremiah would make his prayers shorter. Better yet, she wished that his company would be sent way up to Scotland to fight, so that he would get home less often. She tried to count her blessings by remembering that at least he wasn't home *much* of the time as it was, and that now Will would be gone too; but that didn't help much—especially after the unwelcome reminder that she was supposed to marry Will some day. She wouldn't! She just *wouldn't*! Her back stiffened, but her heart sank with the awful fear that they might be able to force her into it. They always did win, she remembered bleakly. In more than two years, she had never got her own way once, about anything!

In the middle of the prayer, Lark made a small private vow. She would escape her horrid, mean relations one way or another. And when she did, she would always have her own way for the rest of her life!

Behind Lark, Aunt Judith looked hard at the back of her problem niece. The white-capped head was properly lowered, and the nape of the childish neck looked very vulnerable between the neat brown braids, but that narrow back was much too straight for anything like humility of spirit. Mistress Talbot glanced over the children's heads at her husband, who was quick to take the hint.

"Look upon Elizabeth, Oh Lord," he commanded. Lark stiffened slightly. "Thou knowest how I have tried to lead her from the ungodliness of her early training. Chasten her stubborn and rebellious spirit, and bring her in repentance to Thy feet so that she may become worthy to receive the name Submit."

Lark immediately hardened her heart against God. She had no desire at all to be renamed Submit, not even for salvation and heaven. In any event, it seemed quite unlikely that she was one of the Elect, and if God predestined everyone to salvation or damnation before they were even born, Lark really couldn't see any point in worrying much about her rebellious spirit at this late date. On the other hand, if it turned out that Uncle Jeremiah was wrong about God, and her own family right, and God didn't predestine people at all, then there was even less point in letting herself earn such a horrid name as Submit. Lark concealed a very logical mind behind her childish face.

She did not share this particular bit of logic with her uncle, however. Such confidences, she had discovered, invariably led to long and uncomfortable lectures and more praying. Questions of any kind were most upsetting to Uncle Jeremiah—especially the kind of questions that occurred to Lark. So she raised her round eyes to his with the blank, newborn look of a baby.

Her uncle was by now almost convinced that his niece was not really rebellious at all, but merely not quite bright. He wondered, as he ended his prayer and arose, what arrangements God made for such unfortunates. Then he hastily pushed the disturbing question aside and wondered instead if she could really be shaped into a proper wife for Will-of-God by the time she grew up.

By the time she grew up . . . He seated himself at the head of the supper table and glanced again at his niece as she took her place along the side bench with his own six. She didn't seem to be growing at all, he discovered. She looked no larger than when he had first brought her, a small and fiercely rebellious eleven-year-old, to his home. And she somehow looked even smaller now, perhaps because his own sturdy, red-cheeked offspring were considerably larger now . . . Jeremiah found this disturbing. Neighbors might think he didn't feed her enough.

"You're a puny child, Elizabeth," he remarked reprovingly. "You ought to eat more."

His entire family looked at him with astonishment. "Eat more?" echoed his wife. "But husband, she already eats nearly as much as Will-of-God!"

"She does?" Jeremiah looked with surprise at his oldest son, who nodded a trifle resentfully. "Well, then . . ." He dismissed the subject. Apparently it was God's Will that Elizabeth remain puny, no doubt as punishment for having been born and raised in a non-Puritan family.

Lark was demurely silent, with her eyes on her plate and her ears on her uncle's conversation. It was the best way to learn about what was going on in England—and Lark was vitally interested in what went on in England. If only the young King Charles and the Royalists and the Scots could defeat Cromwell after all, Mother and Father could come back from exile and she could go back home to them. She blinked hard, for her eyes often got blurred with tears when she thought of her mother and father. She hastily pulled her thoughts back and listened.

"Is it true, husband," asked Aunt Judith worriedly, "that that dreadful young Charles is bringing the wild savage Scots in an army to invade us? The neighbors say we're all likely to be murdered in our beds."

"Aye, he's invaded true enough, may Satan fly off with him!" Uncle Jeremiah glowered. "But there's no danger here so near the south coast, wife. Cromwell is following close behind, and more of our army is heading north. The Scots will be crushed before they get as far as Manchester." He dismissed Charles Stewart as of no consequence and turned to look at his niece again, dissatisfied. "There's no color in her cheeks," he pointed out critically.

Lark's creamy cheeks just weren't of the pink-and-white variety. But she now saw a chance to pass her detested dull gray skirt and bodice down to Patience and perhaps fall heir to the slightly less drab brown one that Honour was outgrowing. "Gray always makes me look pale," she explained artlessly, thinking of the bright wildflower colors she used to wear at home.

Uncle Jeremiah sometimes had a disconcerting habit of seeming to guess her thoughts. "I suppose you'd like a frock of scarlet taffeta?" he suggested dryly. "I fear the Devil is still at work in you, Elizabeth. I would suggest rather a walk in the fresh air for your cheeks. If your aunt doesn't need you this afternoon, you may walk into the village for me, to deliver a note to the parson."

"Yes, sir," said Lark humbly, careful not to show her delight. There seemed to be a general rule among Puritans that if one enjoyed something, it must be bad for the soul, and vice versa.

A little later she paced sedately out of the weathered stone house and down the lane, hardly able to believe her good fortune. A walk all the way to the village, out in the enchanting summer sunshine, without a critical cousin in sight! She wanted to skip and run and sing, but she prudently waited for that until she was safely around the turn of the road and into the wood. Instead she gave her best imitation of a lark—a trick her big brother had taught her in honor of her nickname.

The forest was magical today. Silver-trunked beech trees soared upward to make a flecked roof of green and blue, and there were emerald cushions of moss at their feet. Squirrels frolicked fearlessly, and a yaffingale sang, and it was perfectly ridiculous to suppose that a God who made all this did not love beauty and color and joy and song.

Lark sang.

But she stopped when she came near the steep-roofed cottage at the edge of the wood. It was a very nice cottage, set in the midst of an herb garden—but it was the home of Mistress Tillyard, and Lark was a trifle nervous about that old lady. She had, for one thing, a long nose and chin, and deep-set eyes beneath beetling brows, and she brewed potions of herbs. She might easily have been a witch if she had not, instead, been one of the most outspoken and strict Puritans for miles around. Lark wasn't sure which of the two was more alarming.

It was fortunate that she stopped singing when she did, for as the road entered the clearing, Lark saw Mistress Tillyard coming out of her cottage.

2
The Lark Flies

Lark's footsteps faltered slightly. Mistress Tillyard was walking with the brisk air of someone who might be going to the village, too, and Lark did not in the least want her lovely walk spoiled by this formidable old woman. Still, her mother had fixed a firm notion of proper manners in her head, and she felt that she could neither rush past nor hang back and hide.

Moreover, Mistress Tillyard had paused by her gate, and was definitely looking at Lark. She even beckoned to her with a bony forefinger. There was no help for it. Lark went along up to her and curtseyed.

"You're Jeremiah Talbot's niece, Elizabeth Lennox, aren't you?" demanded Mistress Tillyard.

"Yes, Ma'am," agreed Lark, faintly surprised. Not knowing what else to say, she prudently said nothing.

"We'll walk along together if you're going to the village," commanded the old woman, and set out at a surprisingly nimble pace. "I've been wanting to talk to you, especially the last day or so. How do you like living with your uncle, by the way? Does he treat you well?"

Lark tactfully hid her surprise and ignored the first part of the question. "He treats me the same as his own children," she said truthfully, "except that he prays about me a little more often." She refrained from adding that in her opinion some of her cousins could have well done with extra prayers, for Will-of-God bullied all the smaller ones, Faithful was selfish, Temperance had a sharp tongue, and little Patience was a shocking crybaby and tell-tale.

The old woman chuckled. "But he still hasn't made a Puritan of you, has he?" Then she chuckled again as Lark turned a blank face to her. "So that's your armor, is it?"

"I don't know what you mean," said Lark, looking blanker than ever.

"Your expression," Mistress Tillyard explained, suddenly sounding quite kind. "We all need something to hide behind when we feel alarmed or not sure of ourselves. It might be anger or tears, or sarcasm, or laughter, or a shrug. Yours is that look of affable imbecility. It's quite effective, you know. Makes you look pitifully young. . . . How old are you, really?"

Lark eyed Mistress Tillyard with considerable alarm. How could she know so much about a person she had scarcely spoken to before now? "Thirteen," she admitted reluctantly.

"Good. Don't remind people of it, though. The younger and more helpless you look, the better your defense. It suits you, with that short face and those wide eyes." She stopped in the road and turned to lift Lark's chin with a finger and study her face. "Widow's peak," she murmured. "Wide across the eyes and cheekbones, short chin—like a fat heart lopped off at the bottom. It's not a bad face, my dear. It hides originality and independence of mind."

Lark blinked. She had never been particularly conscious of having originality and independence of mind, but now it had been brought to her attention, she saw quite clearly that it was so. The discovery pleased her. She began to feel affection for the strange old woman.

Mistress Tillyard dropped Lark's chin and continued walking. "Tell me, poppet, what do you hear of your own family?" she asked.

Lark began to get into the spirit of this surprising conversation. "Practically nothing," she said sadly. "Sometimes they write, but Aunt Judith or Uncle Jeremiah keep their letters and just tell me what they think I should know. And I haven't heard anything at all about my sister." She paused and looked at Mistress Tillyard, who was looking as interested as if she knew Lark's family.

"Your sister?" she prompted gently.

"She married a Scot," explained Lark. "And so of course she went to live in Scotland. And I *think* she's still safe there, but I don't know, because I haven't heard anything for more than two years." She stared at the ground, feeling as forlorn as she always did when she allowed herself to think about these things.

"Yes, she's still there," said Mistress Tillyard as calmly as if she went around dropping thunderbolts every day of the year. "Things are quite peaceful in those remote glens of the Highlands. She has a baby, and she sends you her love, and wishes you could be with her."

Lark had stopped dead in the road and was simply staring. "I—I—How—"

"How do I know?" The old woman smiled toothlessly. "Oh, I have my ways, and it will be safer if you don't know them. But the message is quite recent, poppet. It didn't come in one of those expensive letters that can be delayed for months, and perhaps never arrive at all. That's all I can tell you, so be content."

Lark walked on in dazed silence, and Mistress Tillyard, looking at the radiant small face, was pleased. She would have been less pleased had she known that Lark had just, at that moment, definitely decided to go to Scotland.

It was not Mistress Tillyard's fault that she underestimated Lark's initiative. It had been very shrewd of her to see as much as she had in that babyish looking face. And there was nothing in the least sudden about Lark's decision. She had merely been biding her time, all along, until the right time should come. It would never do just to run away at random. She must have a definite place to run *to*, and the news from Cecily was all she needed.

Although it took Lark only three seconds to decide to go to Scotland, it took a full three weeks to plan and prepare, for Lark was the sort of person who could plan wildly impossible things in a perfectly practical way. She surprised Aunt Judith by her industry in finishing the new warm brown cloak that was for next winter, and then she talked herself into Honour's brown skirt and bodice. It was, she pointed out, so short for Honour that a positively indecent amount of ankle showed, and what would the neighbors think?

Her astonishing appetite became even more astonishing, for she began saving everything that would keep, and hiding it in her apron pocket to be stored later in her little tin box that was hidden in the corner of the shed. She also helped herself, a little at a time, to raisins and nuts and other dried things from the cupboards, explaining to her conscience that it wasn't really stealing, but only borrowing in advance on the future meals she wouldn't be here to eat, and in the long run it would still save Aunt Judith a great deal on food. Her conscience, of course, would never dream of taking so much as a farthing of money, but she did have two shillings, fivepence halfpenny of her very own, that had been in her pocket when she left home.

Next Lark began getting up in the middle of the night, explaining to the sleepily indignant Temperance, whose bed she shared, that she was off to the night chamber, or to get a drink of water. After the first week Temperance no longer bothered to grumble, and in two weeks she didn't even wake up when her cousin slipped out of the high four-poster.

Finally, Lark counted the steps from her bed to the stairs, and all the way to the garden door, memorizing every creaky spot. She even practiced walking the chosen route with her eyes shut, until one day Aunt Judith caught her at it.

"What on earth are you doing, Elizabeth?"

Lark opened her eyes to their widest, remembering Mistress Tillyard's advice. "I just wanted to see what it would be like if I were blind," she invented, and then bowed her head meekly while Aunt Judith pointed out at great length that she would do much better to be thinking of God, and whether her soul were in a State of Grace.

But after three weeks Lark began to realize she was taking rather more time to prepare than she really needed, and that the reason for this was because she was a little afraid. Lark couldn't bear being a coward. She would rather, she thought, be downright wicked. And so she decided to set out that very night.

She lay still and tense on the edge of the bed for what seemed hours. One by one Honour and Temperance and Patience stopped whispering and began breathing deeply and regularly. She waited. Presently a muffled growling began from down the hall: Aunt Judith snoring. Her snores were not nearly as loud and varied as Uncle Jeremiah's, Lark reflected, but they were impressive all the same. Had she waited long enough? Yes, it must be safe now. She couldn't bear to hold still a moment more!

She inched her way out of bed, freezing where she was and holding her breath while Temperance grunted and turned over in her sleep. She breathed and moved again, and then quietly scooped up her clothes, shoes, and work bag, which she had laid conveniently near the door. She moved forward—

And then the sleepy voice of Patience inquired peevishly from the other bed whether that was Elizabeth, and where she was going.

"Where do you think I'm going?" hissed Lark, in a panic lest the others wake up, too. She had never disliked Patience as much as she did now.

Patience sniffed resentfully, muttering that Elizabeth needn't be so rude, need she, and just wait until Mother heard about it in the morning, and *then* she'd see.

"Oh, hush," Lark whispered, and then quickly slipped out of the door before Patience could answer back. But she stood there for a moment, listening. If Patience did decide to create a fuss . . . But there was silence again.

Lark swallowed hard, and began to follow the dark route she had traveled so many times in practice. Down the hall she crept, keeping to the right side because of the squeaky board on the left. Then down the stairs—counting—skipping the second and seventh steps—and along the tiled lower hall, which had, thank goodness, no creaks at all. She snatched the warm winter cloak from its peg and hurried into the big kitchen, which still glowed faintly from the direction of the huge fireplace. The first step was accomplished!

She stood still for an instant, panting a little from excitement, hardly daring to believe it. Then she hastily dressed, one ear cocked toward the stairs, filled with a splendid sense of adventure well started. After that she regarded her voluminous nightgown with deep perplexity. What was she to do with it? She couldn't just leave it here to be found at the crack of dawn. Finally she simply stuffed it into her workbag along with a clean collar and cap, her comb, and her small silken purse with her precious coins.

The garden door unbolted easily, and she was out in the summer darkness and across the vegetable garden to the little shed, where she took out her hoard of food and put that in on top of the nightgown. The bag was distinctly bulky by now, but she could worry about that later. Now it was time to put as much distance as possible between herself and Aunt Judith, and do it before dawn. Thank goodness Uncle Jeremiah and Will had gone back to the army! Lark wasn't at all sure she would have the courage to go at all if they had been here to start searching for her.

She flickered like a shadow through the garden gate, and started off on the small road that led away from the village to the north. All she had to do was keep on going north until she reached Scotland, and then she could begin to ask about Cameron country, where Cecily lived. She set out cheerfully.

Presently she felt less cheerful. The land stretched blackly around her, and it occurred to her for the first time that she was not at all sure how far it was to Scotland from Fordingbridge-near-Salisbury, which was the nearest town she knew. Suppose it was as much as a hundred miles! The thought was daunting. Would two shillings, fivepence halfpenny take care of inns, and more food when hers ran out, for all that way? Moreover, there might be danger with the country all upset about the Scottish invasion. Suppose she met a robber or goblin or evil spirit or Gypsy, or something?

By the time she reached the edge of a very dark-looking wood, she was definitely wondering if this was such a good idea, after all. Perhaps she had been too hasty? It was not too late to change her mind. She paused, peering into the blackness of the forest, considering. But then it dawned on her that she was frightened, and if she turned back now she would dislike herself forever for being a coward, and even meeting a goblin would be better than that. Taking a deep breath, she marched into the woods.

After a few minutes it seemed less dark and alarming.

Her eyes got used to it, and presently a moon came up and filtered through the trees. She went on and on, though she was getting a little tired. The woods ended, and the road found its way to a river and ran along beside it. Lark had a drink and resisted the temptation to eat all of her food. She was extremely hungry.

When the sky to the northeast began to gray, she saw that the road was still leading her northward. When the sun came up, she found a patch of trees and underbrush. There she hid herself amid long grass and elderberry bushes, and curled up for a nap. She felt rather pleased with herself. She would stay hidden during the day, when Faithful or some of the neighbors might be searching for her, and she did not think they would find her here. Aunt Judith would doubtless think she had gone south to the coast, to try to get to France.

Lark made herself more comfortable, stared sleepily up at the tranquil morning sky for a moment, imitated a lark for a bar or two, yawned, and went to sleep.

3
The Rescue

James strode along in full daylight, enjoying life. He had been in Dorset and Hampshire for the last three weeks or so, and now was heading northward again, sorry only that he hadn't been able to stop for another visit with Mistress Tillyard. She was not only a delightful person, but she had taught him a great deal about passing as a staunch Puritan. That came in handy, these days. James put more faith in this knowledge than in the tinker's tools which he now was carrying to distract suspicion.

James fondly hoped that no one would ask him to repair a pan or anything. If they did, he was going to say that he was just taking them to his father near Shrewsbury as a gift from an elderly uncle. He wouldn't have bothered with them at all, but the squire near Corfe Castle had been very insistent, and James hadn't wanted to hurt his feelings. He had worked very hard on that squire, who had gallantly supported Cromwell until the execution of King Charles I two years ago. There, like many other Englishmen, the squire had drawn the line. Beheading one's king—however badly the king might have behaved—was, he felt, going too far. He had withdrawn himself from the Parliament army, returned to his home, and brooded. It was one of James's tasks to visit such men and try to bring them around to the point of view that perhaps Cromwell was becoming an even worse tyrant than he claimed Charles had been, and that young Charles should be accepted as King.

Persuading people of this was not easy these days, with young Charles actually leading a Scottish army into England. In fact, it was exceedingly difficult. Even Royalists were beginning to mutter that now it was Charles who was going too far, and that even Cromwell was better than the Scots.

Still, James was very persuasive. Although he was only eighteen, his candid brown eyes and logic were very convincing, and the squire had been deeply impressed—especially when he found out that Charles was practically a prisoner of the Scots, and had no choice in the matter, and that it was up to loyal Englishmen to free him and send the Scots back home with a flea in their ears. It was very pleasant to feel that he was doing something really helpful for Charles, who was only three years older than himself, and who had already had more misfortune than James had seriously dreamed of.

He strolled along by the side of the river in the radiant sunshine. Around the next bend, a lark broke into song. James smiled and then frowned. It wasn't a lark, although it was an excellent imitation. The sweet fluting broke into a gay Cavalier song in a girl's voice.

> "I prithee send me back my heart,
> Since I cannot have thine;
> For if from yours you will not part,
> Why then shouldst thou have mine?"

James's eyebrows flew upwards. A Cavalier song in Puritan England? What could the lark, whoever it was, be thinking?

The lark song began again after the verse, and James breathed more easily. But then the reckless words came in again, and a moment later there was a man's angry voice.

It would have been sensible of James to avoid investigating a scene which could so easily get himself and his king's work into difficulties. But James was not the sort to avoid difficulties. He was a Cavalier himself—and he could never resist adventure. He hurried around the knoll at the river bend to see what was happening.

The lark turned out to be a small girl dressed in brown. She was looking with alarm at a thick-set young man, also in Puritan dress, who advanced toward her angrily. Her brother, no doubt, and none of James's business. But an instant later he made it his business. For the young man gave the little girl a clout on the ear that knocked her to the ground, and James saw red.

But when James saw red it was always with great calmness. Moreover, he did not believe in resorting to violence unless it became necessary. He sauntered over to where the young man was looming over the lark, and regarded them with interest. The lark, he observed, was sitting up, apparently more scared than hurt.

The young man turned his stocky figure toward James. "If this is your sister," he growled, "you had best discipline her. She was singing a vile, ungodly song."

So the young man didn't know the lark, after all! James raised his eyebrow. "I have never heard of a Commandment that said 'Thou shalt not sing,' " he observed mildly. "However, I do seem to remember a passage in the Bible that says 'Judge not, that ye be not judged.' "

The young man glowered, and James perceived that he was not much impressed. Puritans much preferred the Old Testament to the New. He tried again. "Or there is the Proverb: Cursed is he who smiteth the young and helpless," he added.

The young man looked baffled. Clearly he had never heard this proverb, which was not surprising, since James had just made it up on the spur of the moment. Encouraged, James put his literary skill to work once more. "Or Isaiah," he continued pleasantly. "He who raiseth his arm against one of these, my children, him the Lord hateth and shall cast into eternal fire."

The young man by now looked distinctly uneasy, and James might have left well enough alone. But he had got into the spirit of the thing, and could not resist going on. "Or Ezekiel," he said. "He who is a great lout with the face of a pig and the mind of a weasel, let him keep his hands to himself."

At that, the great lout gave a bellow of rage and threw himself at James; and in the twinkling of an eye a brisk battle was in progress.

Lark scrambled to her feet to avoid being trampled, and tried to decide what to do. Whoever the brown young man was, he was doing battle for her, and she felt a great love for him. However, it seemed that love would not be of much help at the moment, for the other man was much larger. More active assistance was needed, so Lark leaped at the back of the lout and clung, her feet locked firmly about his legs.

The lout staggered and tried to shake her off. James glanced at her and yelled for her to get away, and in that instant received a large fist right in his eye. After that he was too busy to take much notice. Lark clung until she was thrown off, and then came back for more. This time she managed to find a section of arm, and—being quite unversed in the rules of polite fighting—bit it. The lout yelled, Lark flew off again, and the two men rolled to the ground.

Lark, panting from the effort, saw clearly that Her Hero was going to be severely beaten if she didn't do something more constructive than biting. Heroism alone could not always make up for sheer physical force. But what could she do? She picked up a stone, but they were rolling around so much that she was afraid of hitting the wrong one. Then the fight rolled to the very edge of the bank that overhung the river.

Lark hurled her small self with all her might at the tangle, and the three of them went over the bank and into the river with a huge splash.

Things were extremely confused for the next few minutes. The current at that spot was surprisingly strong for such a mild looking river, and Lark felt herself turned over and swirled under the water and away from the bank. She could swim a tiny bit—more than most girls—but not, she felt sure, well enough for this. It was all she could do to struggle to the surface and take a deep breath before she went under again, and she found herself thinking that Uncle Jeremiah must have been right after all, and God was taking His vengeance upon her.

Then she felt herself caught up in a strong arm, and her face was out of the water again, and a voice said, "Just hold still, little girl, and I'll have you safe in a minute."

Lark obeyed, realizing that perhaps God wasn't angry after all, and that she was once more being saved by the fine young man, whom she trusted completely. A few minutes later he had found a low place on the bank, heaved her up so that she could catch hold of a bush, climbed up the bank himself, and was lifting her easily to a sunny, grassy place well away from that frightening river. They looked around for the enemy and saw him, some distance down the river, scrambling ashore on the other side. They both gave sighs of relief and looked at each other.

Lark saw that although he wore cropped hair and plain homespun breeches and jerkin like any Puritan, there was laughter in his brown eyes . . . or at least in the one which was not rapidly closing and turning purple. Because of that and one or two other things, she did not think he was any more a dyed-in-the-wool Puritan than she was. She did not, for that matter, really care if he were. She liked him tremendously, and he had saved her twice.

James saw a baby face with round, widely spaced eyes the color of green moss seen through peaty brown water. There was an enchanting snub nose, and a short round chin, and an unexpected dimple just under one corner of her mouth when she gave him a sudden and delightful smile. A charming child, he thought. James liked children, and had always wished for a little sister.

"Thank you," said Lark earnestly. "He was ever so much bigger than you, and I think you're just terribly brave and noble."

"Not at all, poppet," said James. He sat down on the grass beside her, feeling quite fatherly, and took her hands in his to see if she were chilled from her sudden bath. They were small hands, quite warm and alive in his, although she was dripping wet. He smiled back at her. "We'll have to get you home and into dry clothes," he said. "Where do you live, little lark?"

Lark's eyes widened. "My family always called me Lark!" she said delightedly. "How did you know?"

"I didn't," said James. "But you were singing like one —and please don't sing that Cavalier song again unless you are perfectly sure no one is around. I can't think where you learned it, to begin with. Now, where is your home, my poppet?"

"I haven't any," Lark told him. And looking into his nice but startled eyes, she felt that he was a friend. "You see," she confided, "I've run away from my wicked uncle."

James's eyebrows raised halfway up his forehead and he swallowed a little. He supposed he would have to coax her, calm her down, and then take her back himself. But the first thing was to get her dry. "You're shivering," he pointed out. "And I left my cloak back there where we fell into the river."

"I left mine there too," Lark remembered. "And my bag." They got up and started back up the river bank. "What is your name?" she asked presently, feeling that they really knew each other now except for that minor point.

James hesitated for just an instant. The child clearly

came from a Puritan home, and it was as well if she didn't know his whole name, but he didn't want to lie to her. "I don't think we need to be formal now, do you?" he suggested with an engaging smile. "Why don't you just call me James? And what is your name?"

Lark smiled back cheerfully. "Lark is what I like best to be called, so you can go right on calling me that," she announced. And then, at his disconcerted look, she added candidly, "You see, if you knew my right name and where I lived, you might think it was your duty to send me back, but this way your conscience needn't bother you."

James stared. His experience with small girls had not led him to expect this kind of shrewdness—especially not from such an innocent-faced lark-child as this. He found it extremely confusing.

"But you'll have to go home—I mean back to your uncle—sooner or later," he explained kindly. "After all, where else can you go?"

"To Scotland," Lark told him as casually as if she had said "across the road."

"Awp!" said James inadequately, and then became speechless.

"You see," Lark explained, "my uncle brought his soldiers and stole me away from my mother and father, and then my family was put out of their house and they had to go to France and be exiles, and I can't go to them because I haven't a boat. But my sister is in Scotland, and I don't need a boat to get there, so I'm going to live with her."

"Scotland!" echoed James. "My sweet Lark, you can't possibly go to Scotland! It's out of the question. You mustn't even consider such a thing! You have no idea—You must go back to your uncle at once. At least you'll be safe there."

Lark shook her head. The independence and originality Mistress Tillyard had seen were very much in evidence, and her chin, though small, showed possibilities of unbelievable stubbornness. James argued in vain all the way back to where they had left their things on the sunny river bank, and then decided to postpone the battle until they were dry.

He looked at the bulging workbag which lay by her cloak. "I don't suppose you have a change of clothing in there," he suggested without much hope.

"I have a clean collar and cap," said Lark, "and my nightgown. I could put that on while my clothes get dry. It's such a hot day that it shouldn't take long."

"Nightgown?" James echoed dubiously. It seemed an odd thing to be taking to Scotland—and he wasn't sure it was proper for her to wear it right out in the open air like this. He said so.

Lark looked at him. "Well, it's the only other thing I've got," she pointed out. "And I don't see why it isn't perfectly respectable. After all, it covers just as much of me as my skirt and bodice do."

Defeated by this logic, James draped both of their cloaks tent-like over a willow sapling, and then obligingly turned his back and watched out to see that no more great louts were coming along while Lark changed. When he turned around and came back, she looked even younger and more vulnerable than before in the full white folds of the nightgown, with a snowy ruff tied demurely under her chin.

Half of her hair, released from its braid, fell over her shoulders into her lap and spilled down to the ground.

"It will dry faster," explained Lark, beginning on the other braid. "Are you hungry? I am. There's some food in my bag."

James guessed that it was her only food, meant to last all the way to Scotland, and he was deeply touched at such generosity. But he could hardly refuse—and in any case, he was going to see her back to her uncle safely—so he brought out the nuts and raisins and cheese. They ate together, sitting face to face in the high warm grass. Her hair, as it dried, fascinated him. It was straight and thick, curling just a trifle at the ends, which fell below her hips. And it was an odd light brown with a silvery sheen to it, as if it were being seen in the moonlight. A lovely child! Not pretty, exactly, but lovely.

He reluctantly broke the contented silence with a return to the disputed matter of Scotland. "Believe me, little Lark," he said. "You can't possibly make a trip like that. It's too far and too hard, and there are too many dangers. Soldiers and bandits and hunger and cold—and I doubt if you would have nearly enough food or money to get a quarter of the way. You'd be stopped and questioned even if you didn't starve, and besides, there are two armies between here and Scotland, and you might end up right in the middle of a battle."

"But I *have* to go," Lark said simply. "I'd rather face all of those things than go back. Besides," she remembered, shuddering, "just think what my uncle would do!" She deliberately stopped there, leaving James to imagine far worse things than Uncle Jeremiah would probably actually do to her—although the reality would be quite bad enough, even at best.

James could see in his mind the welts that would appear on Lark's fragile skin; and her small bones—bones like a bird—in the callous grip of a brutal and sadistic uncle. He could feel the humiliation, which he knew instinctively would hurt this child even more than pain. He groaned. What on earth was he to do?

Lark glanced up at him from under long lashes. The look of a trusting babe was on her face. "Where are *you* going, James?" she asked.

James looked at her helplessly.

4
The Wish

"It's out of the question!" said James for at least the fiftieth time. They were walking along a pleasant path in the general direction of Salisbury.

Lark smiled at him. They were heading roughly northward, which was the right direction for Scotland, and she felt sure that James would take care of her, so she was not inclined to argue the point just now.

James felt that he wasn't getting anywhere. "Why don't you wait until after the battle?" he asked, humoring her. "Then if King Charles wins, your parents can come back and get you, and everything will be all right."

Lark had thought of that, too, of course. But she wasn't going back now. She changed the subject. "Is King Charles really our king now?" she asked. "Uncle Jeremiah said not."

"I'm not sure, myself," James admitted, forgetting

her extreme youth for the moment. "I suppose it depends on how you look at it. Some say he became king the minute his father was beheaded, because he was heir to the throne; but others say he has to be properly crowned. Of course he *was* crowned in Scotland last winter, but I'm not sure if that counts for England or not. You see, poppet, England and Scotland were always two separate countries with two rulers until Queen Elizabeth died, and then King James became ruler of both countries. Then each country split into two sides when the civil war began: for the king and against him. And you know the Royalists lost and Charles I had his head chopped off; only now the Scots have decided they want Charles II, so they're invading England with him, to make him king of both countries and throw out Cromwell, and—" He paused, feeling that he had got much too complicated for a small girl. As a matter of fact, it was a bit muddled even for him.

But Lark was less confused than he supposed. "Well, then," she decided, going straight to the heart of the matter with what James considered admirably straightforward logic. "Charles *is* king, isn't he?"

"As far as I'm concerned," agreed James, smiling at her. Trust a child to see the main point, he thought. Babes didn't bother with all the little side issues that were so apt to muddle grownups. . . . Lark, for her part, was thinking how clever James was to be able to present all sides of the question so clearly. She smiled back at him admiringly, and encouraged him to explain some more things.

"I thought the Scots were on Cromwell's side." She frowned. "Didn't they capture the first King Charles themselves, and then give him to Cromwell to be executed?"

"They did," James agreed bleakly. "But you see they have never really been on any side but their own, and they're so narrow and ultra-Puritan that even Cromwell thinks they go too far. And when they found that Cromwell wasn't going to let them run both countries, they got young Charles to come back from Holland and be crowned, so they could turn around and fight Cromwell. Only then they started quarreling among themselves—trust the Scots for that—and made Charles sign all sorts of humiliating things, so that he said he thought he'd better apologize for having been born."

"Why does he let them do that to him?" asked Lark, going again to the heart of the matter.

James shrugged. "Well, for one thing, they *have* him. And I expect he hopes, as the rest of us do, that if he can beat Cromwell, then all England can unite and settle the Scots. The only trouble is," he added gloomily, "that a lot of Englishmen who might have supported Charles by himself have turned against him for bringing in the Scots." He sighed, for optimist though he was, he could see nothing but disaster ahead.

In addition, James now had a new problem of his own. He looked down at Lark and wondered what on earth he was going to do with her. He couldn't take her back, since she wouldn't tell him her name or where she came from. He couldn't take her on the king's business, since this would be dangerous both for the cause and for Lark. And he couldn't just abandon her. The only possibility was to leave her with friends along the way. He began to feel quite elderly and burdened.

"What is that place?" asked Lark, who knew very little about geography except that Scotland was to the north. She pointed to a slender spire that rose above roofs and treetops some little distance ahead.

"Salisbury," replied James, looking at it doubtfully. He would have felt fairly comfortable passing through the town as a tinker of obviously Puritan convictions, or even as a lad taking tinker's tools to his father. But the presence of Lark, he felt, was going to complicate matters. He stopped near a large oak tree, looked up it speculatively, and began to climb.

"What are you doing?" asked Lark with great interest.

"Hiding my tinker's tools," he informed her, doing so. "A tinker wouldn't have his little sister along with him," he explained with a rather wry grin when he got back down to earth. "You're my little sister, in case you didn't know, and I'm taking you to stay with dear old Aunt Prudence, who needs you to help about the house. She lives in—um—oh, near Tilshead will do." And he concealed a very small sigh, so as not to hurt the child's feelings. It was true that she was complicating his life and work in a most distracting way, but that wasn't her fault, was it?

Lark was nodding happily at this splendid story, and putting on her cap and collar and a sober and holy look for the occasion. It was a slightly different role from the one she had used for Uncle Jeremiah, she decided, and rather a challenge. For she must be completely convincing in her part, without allowing James to notice what a good actress she was. Lark had no real doubt of her ability to meet the challenge. She had, so her own family frequently told each other, inherited the acting ability of both grandparents. And *they* in turn had actually acted in Master Shakespeare's plays way back in the days of Queen Elizabeth.

She slipped a confiding hand into James's strong one—

not merely because her role demanded it, but also because she felt safer that way. James, she firmly believed, would have full control of any situation that might arise.

James himself, having had more experience, was less sure of this. He hid a certain amount of nervousness under a matter-of-fact air as they passed by the neglected cathedral and went on up High Street toward the market square. Not that anyone was likely to see anything unusual about two more brown-clad people on a market day, but he was not at all sure that even a clever little girl like Lark might not happen to say the wrong thing at the wrong time. He hurried past Silver Street, even though Lark craned her neck to stare down it at Poultry Cross. She had never before seen such a thing—a tiny, six-sided open building of carved stone, with a central pillar rising from the top. It looked terribly interesting, but James hurried her on. "It's just the place where people go to buy and sell poultry," he said.

Lark looked deflated. "Chickens and geese!" she muttered in disgust. "They should at least have something *interesting*!"

James laughed and turned up Castle Street. "This leads to Heale House," he murmured when he was sure no one could overhear. "They're good—uh—friends there; I know them. We can stay the night. You understand, poppet, that you must never talk about anything we say or do, or it might turn out most uncomfortably for both of us."

Lark looked at him indignantly. "Haven't I lived with Uncle Jeremiah for two years? And even before that, my grandmother used to chide me when I—" She stopped, thinking it might not be wise to mention that her grandmother used to tell her she prattled too much. Instead, she shifted ground, and chuckled suddenly. "Grandmother isn't very good at holding *her* tongue. Grandfather says she used to have the most awful temper, and she still does sometimes, but not very often. All the same, she can make people listen even without losing her temper."

She peered sideways at James to see if he was interested. He was, so she went on, not knowing that a great deal of his interest was in picking up some clue as to who Lark might be.

"She even makes kings listen to her," Lark told him, her eyes dancing. "She used to get awfully cross at King Charles—the old one, I mean—and once she told him right to his face that he was an idiot."

James couldn't help laughing—especially since his own father had wished more than once to do the same thing. He also made a mental note that anyone who said that sort of thing to a king must be rather important and entitled as well as outspoken. "What did the King do?" he asked.

"He didn't like it very much," Lark admitted. "But then I think he knew she was very loyal to dare to speak to him like that for his own good. Anyhow, everybody knows Gran did the same thing to *his* father—King James, you know—and she even talked back to Queen Elizabeth once, when she was a girl, so it's the sort of thing everybody expects. So King Charles didn't stay angry, but Queen Henrietta was *very* displeased about it."

James chuckled again, feeling that he would like to meet this redoubtable grandmother, and wishing that she might have addressed a few pithy words of advice to young Charles before he went to Scotland. Then he fell silent as they walked along the road curving northward along the

River Avon. Who on earth could Lark be, with a grandmother in royal circles and a Puritan uncle who was a tyrant and an officer under Cromwell? Not that it was unusual for families to be bitterly divided in these wars—but unless Lark was telling whoppers, she belonged to a very important family.

He smiled determinedly. With such a famous grandmother, surely it might not be hard to find out who she was.

"What an unusual person she must be," he remarked blandly. "How surprising that I have never heard the story of her scolding the king! That's the sort of thing that usually gets told all over. What is her name, Lark?"

Lark, not caught out for a moment, gave him a roguish smile and then considered the question seriously. Then she shook her head. "I thought for a minute I might tell you," she explained, "because I should think Grandmother and Grandfather are doing something exciting this very minute to help the new king, and it would be nice if we could find them. Only they're in exile, too, so they're probably doing whatever-it-is in France; and I'm afraid if I tell you who *any* of my family is, you might find out who Uncle Jeremiah is."

She smiled at him again, very sweetly. James ground his teeth.

Heale House spread its lovely old roofs and chimneys amid a stretch of smooth lawns and gardens overlooking the River Avon. James pulled Lark into the shadow of one of the cedar trees which sheltered the gardens and watched carefully for a while before venturing up to the door. One could never be quite sure, in a Royalist home, whether the

Roundheads might have taken possession. His own cousins had lost their house that way last year, and who knew whether his parents might have been put out in the two months since he had seen them last?

But presently he glimpsed a groom he recognized, and after that the travelers found themselves wrapped in hospitality. The widowed and elderly Mistress Hyde seemed to be a busy and hospitable sort of person with bright eyes and several relatives living with her and a great interest in outside affairs. She welcomed James as if he had been at least a nephew.

Lark, who had already assumed that James was a member of her own class, was now sure of it. Moreover, she caught a few phrases here and there which suggested that he was, in some mysterious way, on the king's business. She wasn't in the least surprised. Any king worth his salt would surely have the sense to recognize James as a most remarkable and wonderful person.

But Lark, as she had told James, knew very well how to keep her observations to herself. He never suspected that every word of the cautious conversation, every detail of manner and behavior was being absorbed by the wide-eyed child beside him, and put together into a terrifyingly accurate picture.

James, she saw clearly, was of the nobility, for he was treated as an equal here, and even was lent a suit of fine azure taffeta with a lace collar. He was perfectly at ease, too, at the fine dinner table set with silver and linen, and tended by stiff, liveried servants.

It was also clear that James and Mistress Hyde guessed the same thing about Lark, and for the same reasons. Although it had been more than two years since she had been in such gracious surroundings, she slipped into them as easily as a fish into water.

The talk at dinner was, of course, all of the Scottish army which was presumably still on its way southward along the west of England. As far as anyone knew, Cromwell was still following, and there would surely be a battle. But the others were more optimistic about the outcome than James seemed to be.

"Well, I hope you're right," he said at last. "But I still think I'd best get to Shrewsbury as soon as I can to meet—uh—my friend." His eyes flickered briefly at Lark, who knew perfectly well that he was being cautious because of her, but she kept her face carefully blank. "I wonder," James went on, "whether I might ask you to take care of Lark for a little while. I can't very well take her with me."

Lark's mouth dropped open in reproach and outrage. "But I'm going to Scotland!" she protested indignantly.

Everyone looked at her. "Scotland?" they echoed. "Nonsense!" they said kindly, chuckling a little at the very notion. "A child like you can't possibly go to Scotland," they told her indulgently, and dismissed the whole thing as the prattling of a babe.

Lark opened her mouth to announce that she was no child at all, but a young lady of thirteen. Then she remembered Mistress Tillyard's advice, and decided to go on following it, after all. All the same, she wasn't about to give in to this outrageous sort of decision.

"I perfectly understand that James can't take me," she said sadly but with dignity. "But I can still go by myself. I got along quite well for nearly two days before we found each other."

"Yes, and you were in trouble when I found you," retorted James.

"Well, I won't sing that kind of song again, that's all," said Lark reasonably, and James raised his eyes heavenward in despair.

"You can't go, and that's final!" he said.

"You can't stop me unless you lock me up," Lark returned briskly, looking at Miss Hyde. "I don't think you'd like doing that, would you? Besides, I'd raise an awful fuss, you know."

"I certainly wouldn't want to keep you a prisoner," she agreed with great sincerity. "But I shall, if it's necessary to keep you from endangering yourself. I do hope you're old enough to listen to reason, my child. You're clearly from a fine family, and I feel responsible for your well-being. And you know you simply cannot go wandering over the countryside alone, especially in times like these. I shall be happy to keep you here as my guest, and to write to your sister in Scotland, telling her you're safe with me."

Lark saw that she was being out-argued, and it was time to take another tack—especially since she couldn't think of any answers to these reasonable arguments. She smiled in what she hoped was a sweet and childish way. "Mother always said I must never argue with my elders, and especially at the dinner table," she said, looking dismayed at her own bad manners. "I mustn't say anything more, must I?"

Everyone smiled at her kindly, under the mistaken impression that she had given up her silly notion about Scotland. James felt a mixture of relief and pain, but mostly relief. He intended to be on his way the first thing in the morning, and when Lark awoke and found him gone, she might not understand why he slipped off without saying goodbye. He hated to hurt her, and he hoped she would understand some day, but it would be a great load off his mind, too.

He should have known her well enough, even after this short time, to suspect that she had given in much too easily.

Although James was up at dawn, Lark was up well before dawn. She had found a quill and ink in her bedroom the night before, and written a brief note explaining that she had to go to Scotland. In the early hours of the morning she got up, dressed, and slipped quietly out of the house. She had no chance, this time, to make mental notes of things like squeaky boards, but it turned out that in this fine house there were not very many, anyway. The front door was not even bolted.

She sighed as she looked around through the blackness. Running away in the dark of night was getting to be a habit, and it was just as dark this time as it had been the last, and she did not know the countryside around here. The only thing to do, of course, was to go along the driveway until she reached the road that had led them from Salisbury, and then continue northward on it. She set off.

It was very lonely traveling by herself, and not as much fun as the first time. She had got used to James. She trudged on, as the sky slowly turned gray and then apricot. And then, just before sunrise, she came to a crossroad and stopped.

Across the way, to her left, stood a circle of gigantic stones, many of them lying on their sides, but some of them erect, with others balanced across their tops like giant's tables. Lark stared. She had heard of this place. It was called Stonehenge. Her father had said it was old beyond imagining, and that no one knew who built it or where the stones came from (for that kind of stone simply wasn't found within hundreds of miles), or how anyone got them here. Uncle Jeremiah had an explanation for this. He said they came from hell, and Satan had brought them up so that the godless heathen of old could use them for devil worship.

Lark walked a little closer, slowly. She was not quite sure whether or not she believed this last bit, but there was certainly an awesome feeling about the place. It was a little bit frightening. The stones loomed so starkly in the pale light that they seemed to be almost alive, and brooding over the remote past. Still, Lark began to sense as she got closer that it wasn't really an evil feeling. No doubt there was some sort of magic left over from the old days, and perhaps if it wasn't evil it might be good—or at least safe.

She moved slowly to the very center of the circle, and as she stood there, the sun began to rise, the edge of it almost directly over a giant stone that stood by itself like a sentinel some two hundred feet away. The magic got stronger than ever, she thought, and it occurred to her that surely this was the proper time to make a wish.

She made it earnestly, clasping her hands and screwing her eyes shut. Then she went and climbed onto one of the fallen stones, on the side where she could watch the road from Heale House.

And a little more than an hour later, James came in sight.

5

The Blue Dolphin

"I should have taken you right back to Heale House," James said disagreeably.

"You'd have had to drag me every step," retorted Lark, sticking her chin out. "And wouldn't that have been nice? Besides, this isn't your road, and I can walk on it if I want to. Nobody asked you to go with me."

This wasn't strictly true, as she had definitely waited for him and made it rather plain that she wanted his company—but then nobody is very reasonable in the midst of a quarrel. Lark draped her heavy cloak more firmly over her arm and increased her speed with an air of leaving something unwanted behind.

"Oh, *do* try to show some tiny bit of sense for a change!" James growled, keeping up with no difficulty.

"Shan't!" muttered Lark, relieved to find him still with her. She gave a tiny glance sideways to see his expression.

It was very much annoyed, and Lark's own anger ebbed suddenly as it occurred to her that she wasn't being very clever. She should be making James *want* her company, and here she was, instead, being as unpleasant as ever she could.

At precisely the same moment it was occurring to James how idiotic it was to argue like this with a little girl—even a very clever and precocious little girl. He laughed at himself, and Lark joined his laughter with a sense of great relief.

But James sobered after a moment. His good humor was restored, but his problem was as unsolved as ever. What on earth was he to do with her? He *couldn't* go about the king's business saddled with a little girl! On the other hand, neither could he abandon her. He frowned again, and suppressed a brief desire to shake her until she told him her uncle's name and town. It was too late to take her back now, even if she did tell him. And he had a strong feeling that she would not. She really was a most determined child, he reflected, glancing at the smooth brown head with some awe. One would have supposed her Puritan uncle would have made her more tractable.

James couldn't know that Lark's Puritan discipline was part of the trouble. After over two years of sternly enforced obedience, freedom was going to her head. She walked along blissfully, quite drunk with the unaccustomed experience of asserting her own will once again. From now on, she decided dreamily, she would always do so. Not that she meant to be unreasonable, of course, but when she was perfectly sure she was right about a thing (which was usually) she intended to be firm about it—and it seemed that lovely and discriminating people like James then saw her point and gave in. Naturally, she told herself with a sense of great virtue, she would respond by being as helpful and considerate as possible.

She peered up into James's face, which was troubled with his perplexing thoughts. Where next would they place the mythical dear old Aunt Prudence? She had already been moved from Tilshead to Devizes as they made their way northward. Where next? Was he going to have to take Lark all the way to Shrewsbury? What on earth would Doll say? And what would he do with her then?

"I won't interfere in any business you have to do for the King," said Lark, reading his thoughts so uncannily that he stared at her in alarm.

"What made you say a thing like that?" he demanded, and Lark perceived that she had said too much. She put on the expression that Mistress Tillyard had called affable imbecility.

"Or Cromwell or your father or anyone," she prattled on innocently. "I don't know where you're going, really, but if you were having an adventure I think it would be nicer to do something for the King, because we both like him best, don't we?"

James breathed more easily. "You see, it isn't safe to say things like that, even when you think we're alone," he said. "You might get us both into trouble. Remember that song of yours?"

Lark nodded meekly. Whatever James was doing for the king must be extremely important and dangerous, and she loved him more than ever and wished she could help. "All I meant was that I won't interfere with anything you're doing, and whenever you have to go and do it, why

I'll just go on the rest of the way to Scotland by myself, and you mustn't bother or worry or anything."

James groaned.

They walked on for a way in silence, and then Lark looked wistfully at James's pack and at an inn which stood under some cool-looking trees half a mile ahead. She wondered whether they had more food or more money. "Do you suppose," she suggested tentatively, "that we might stop soon for just a tiny bite to eat?"

James followed her glance and read her mind with no difficulty whatever. "Do you mind if we don't stop there, Lark? I happen to know that it's a meeting place for some of the most rigorous Puritans around here, and it might not be very safe for us."

Lark agreed readily, having no desire for any trouble. They walked past the inn with shatteringly saintly faces, and breathed easier when they were well past it and around the next bend of the road. They sat down under a tree, for the weather was still unusually hot, ate the food which James had brought with him from Heale House, and then went on.

It was certainly a lovely day. James kept forgetting the problem which faced him, because it was surprisingly pleasant just talking to Lark. They discovered many tastes in common, such as singing and horses and a great interest in seeing new places and people. They even managed to talk a great deal about their own lives without giving away anything important like last names. For James still had no mind to burden Lark with any knowledge that might be dangerous, and Lark meant to give James no chance to send her back for her own safety.

"When you're being a Puritan and a tinker," inquired Lark presently, "do you talk the same way you are now? Because I should think people would know you were upper class and Cambridge educated and a Cavalier the minute you said two words."

"Oh, no," said James, lapsing into West Country dialect. "Ye see, oi can speak Devon rarely good, look see. Still, Devon do be mostly loyal to king, so," he switched to Yorkshire speech. "So most times, tha see'st, I be a lad fro' th' north, an'—" He broke off, for an alarming thought had come to him. "What a dolt I am!" he exclaimed. "*Your* speech, Lark! It's a miracle it hasn't given us away before now! I'm afraid you're going to have to be deaf and dumb or something."

Lark grinned at him. Not for nothing had she lived two years in Hampshire County. "As folk do say, I mid be one of they foreigners, but not sich a girt one as I were two year gone," she said in her cousins' very tones.

James chuckled, but shook his head. "I can't do Hampshire well enough, and you can't do Yorkshire. We can't be brother and sister, after all—unless—I know! You have *already* been living with dear Aunt Prudence, whom we have just moved back to Lyndhurst, and I'm just fetching you home again, for what with sisters Faith, Truth, and Purity all married and away, Mother needs you."

"All right," agreed Lark, and they laughed together.

At dusk they came to the Blue Dolphin, an inn which James knew, for the host was a secret Royalist and the inn a meeting place and center for messages. Lark stared around with interest as they entered the courtyard, for she had been in an inn only once in her life. A faded blue sign, clearly meant to be a very happy dolphin whisking his tail, swung on an iron rod over the front door. The oaken timbers were almost black with age, and the windows were set deeply into both sides of the heavy door, with the windows of the upstairs rooms set out slightly overhead.

Lark had vaguely expected something a trifle grander in an inn friendly to Royalists, and she was surprised when they stepped through the doorway to find a very plain place indeed. It was darkish, lit only by a few candles which guttered in the draft from the open door, and the orange glow from the huge stone fireplace at the far end. Tables and benches were of solid oak, battered with use, and the men sitting at them were all clad as soberly as Uncle Jeremiah. Lark glanced inquiringly at James, who hastily put a brotherly arm over her shoulders and dug in his fingers in a way that clearly meant for her to keep her mouth shut and her face blank.

At least James hoped that it clearly meant that. For it dawned on him in that instant that he had forgotten to give Lark a very important warning. He should have told her that Royalist sympathies must be kept well underground, for it was highly likely that even here some of the guests were Puritans of the crusading sort, looking around for any hints of a Royalist plot. He squeezed her arm once more, to make the warning more clear, and turned to smile politely at his old friend Walter Hetherington, the host of the inn.

Walter gave him the polite greeting of a stranger, and James followed suit. "Good even, Sir," he said awkwardly. "Ah wonder if tha mought spare a quiet corner for ma wee small sister and masel' for the night."

Only in his eyes did Walter show surprise at James's companion. But before he could answer, one of the gray-clad men at the nearest table spoke up. "What are you thinking of, young man, to bring a little maid into a public tavern?"

James pulled Lark more firmly and protectively to his side, and turned a troubled and apologetic face to his questioner. "It do be no choice of ma own, sir," he explained, "but a matter, tha see'st, of in here or wi' no roof at all, for we do have a bit of a journey yet to get home."

"This is a respectable, God-fearing inn," broke in Walter firmly. "I can find you a quiet corner, young man, and your sister will be quite safe. I do not permit even words which might be unsuitable for innocent ears." He led them to a small table at the far end near the fireplace while James, for the benefit of listening ears, told their little story about Aunt Prudence and the married sisters, and Lark contributed her bit by staring about her with very round eyes.

A savory-smelling haunch of mutton basted on a spit over the fire, turned by a small urchin with a red face. There was also goose pie and roasted carp and a bowl of tansy, clearly made from the freshest eggs and the richest cream. Lark gazed at them with wistful eyes, and James longed to order the best meal in the house for his perpetually hungry small companion, who was really a very good sport about shortened rations. But such a meal would never fit in with his story, so he contented himself with bread and meat. In any case, he knew Walter would quietly fill his pouch with good food during the night, and he wished he could tell that to Lark.

Lark didn't know that James was reading her mind. She would not have dreamed of suggesting expensive food. As it was, she felt uncomfortable to have James paying for her meal, for it didn't seem right, and she was afraid he might have to go hungry later on her account. She determined to eat very little—but in this she failed entirely. It was *so* good, and both James and the host kept filling up her plate.

When they had finished eating, Master Hetherington took Lark to a little nook under the stairs with just enough room for a narrow pallet, and told her that it was her bedroom for the night. James would have a pallet just in front of the nook, and she would be quite safe.

Lark smiled at them both, lay down, and went to sleep almost immediately, for she had not had much sleep the night before, and she was very tired. But she did notice a look that passed between James and the host, and she had just enough time before falling asleep to decide that it was no accident that they had stopped here. James and Master Hetherington clearly knew each other, and were probably working together for the king. Of course she must not let James know that she knew this, for it would doubtless upset him.

When she awoke, daylight was coming in through the diamond-shaped windows and falling rather weakly across the tables—the glass being quite thick and of a faintly greenish tint. James was gone from his pallet, the small boy with the red face was turning the spit just as if he had never left off, and two or three men, yawning a little, were seated at the tables near the front.

Lark stretched, straightened her dress, which was getting quite wrinkled, and scratched vigorously. James's friend might be a good Royalist, she decided, but he ought to change the straw in the pallets more often. She took out her comb, unplaited her hair, and began to work on the tangles. She wasn't worried about James. It never even occurred to her that he would have gone off and left her. He was no doubt talking to Master Hetherington about important matters.

She had just got her hair combed into a long silken waterfall which nearly covered her completely from the hips up, when there was an alarming jingling and clatter from the road outside. A voice shouted an order, and the clatter turned into the courtyard of the Blue Dolphin. Lark paled a little. She knew that sound. She had heard it almost exactly the same way on the day that Uncle Jeremiah had brought his troops to her father's house in Oxford.

She jumped to her feet and peered out of her little nook just as the door was flung open and a group of soldiers stamped in, led by a very grim-faced sergeant. For some reason all the soldiers in Cromwell's army seemed to stamp and scowl and roar. They seemed to feel that it proved something or other about being Godly and Sober and In A State Of Grace.

"Search the place. Back rooms first. No one is to leave!" ordered the sergeant, and then turned to bawl to some other soldiers outside that if they let anyone escape through the back he'd hang the negligent ones. Lark shrank back into her nook, very badly frightened. Where was James? What would happen to them both? Were the Roundheads hunting James in particular, or just Royalists in general, or something else? Would it help things any if she were to escape notice, or would it be worse if they found her hiding? For the moment it seemed best to stay out of sight if possible.

There was a certain amount of uproar going on in the back of the inn, and presently some of the soldiers returned triumphantly with James and Master Hetherington held firmly between them. "We found these two in one of the back storerooms," they announced. "What would they be doing there if they weren't plotting in secret?"

James, even while arranging his face into bewildered innocence, felt his heart sink. They had indeed been caught plotting, and even though nothing had been overheard, the mere possibility of guilt was quite enough these days. He was afraid they couldn't talk their way out of it. And what would happen to poor little Lark, whom he passionately hoped was still hidden in her dark alcove under the stairs? Beside him, he felt Walter's dismay, and heard him speak up in injured defense.

"I don't know what you're talking about!" he declared, alarm and indignation in just the right proportions in his voice. "I'm Walter Hetherington, landlord here, and this is a respectable, God-fearing inn, and I can't think what I've done wrong. There be no law against letting a lad into the back to see could he do some chores."

"Ah suppose it were ma fault," broke in James humbly. "Ah did nobbut ask could ah do a bit o' work, happen like, to pay for part o' food an' lodging, and he kind enow to say ah maught try."

The sergeant shook his head. "We've had reports about this place," he said stubbornly. "A rat's nest of Royalists, with their Devil's plots. I don't believe you, and I'm taking you both along for questioning."

From her dark alcove, Lark saw clearly that suspicion

was as good as proof, and that James was lost, unless . . .

Barely giving herself time to remember her Hampshire dialect, she acted. A small brown figure with streaming hair burst forth from under the stairs, darted under the startled nose of the sergeant, and hurled itself, weeping, upon the dismayed James.

"Oh, brother, brother!" it wailed. "Oh, sir," she appealed to the sergeant, "you do look to be a man of God. Please don't take my brother away, for Mother do be waiting for us, and whatever mid I do without him?"

"Eh?" said the sergeant in great confusion. He looked at the small face, the round terrified eyes in the midst of hair that reminded him somewhat of his own eight-year-old, and his conviction began to waver.

"It be nobbut truth, sir," said James, recovering his wits and pulling Lark's head gently against his chest, where she wept most convincingly. "Ah do be bringing ma wee sister back home to Mother, and us stopped here last night because tha see'st it were growing dark, and her young and tender, an' ah were wishing to save ma siller for t' trip ahead, not wanting ma mother to think me a gormless lad, so ah just askit the landlord here could ah be at a bit o' work, like ah telled thee, and—"

The sergeant silenced him with a gesture. There was a bit of quiet, broken only by Lark's muffled sobs. Walter, knowing a superior act when he saw one, remained silent. The sergeant considered the matter, scowling darkly. It was clear to him that he had missed his prey, for no sane plotter would take a little girl along with him. He looked at his men, who, hardened soldiers that they were, were plainly in sympathy with the pitiful little maid.

"All right, all right," he growled. "Tell your sister to stop her crying, and get on your way. As for you—" He turned to Walter. "I'll just take you along to talk to the Captain, anyway. And these others, too." He indicated the other guests of the inn, who had also been encircled by the soldiers and were standing in the middle of the room looking sour. "Now on your way, boy, before I change my mind."

They went, not even stopping to braid Lark's hair—which, Lark suspected, probably made her look more young and helpless when it was loose, anyway. James did manage to catch Walter's eye once, and was reassured by the very faintest of nods, indicating that he could be most useful by his absence.

Lark was astonishingly calm once they were out from under the Roundheads' eyes, and James looked down at her with awe and a little uneasiness. Either she was frighteningly self-possessed, or else she was being much too quiet for her own good.

Two or three miles further along the road, they found a secluded grove beside a stream, down a bank, and well hidden from passers-by. And at this point Lark's legs, finding that they were no longer required to carry her away from danger, apparently resigned from her body. She sank down on the long grass and began to giggle on a high-pitched note that was quite unlike herself.

James knew at once what was happening. He had half expected it. Seizing her shoulders not too gently, he shook her until she stopped laughing and began to sob. He dunked her face in the cool stream, and then he let her put her head on his knee and cry for a while. When she raised it and demanded food, he decided quite accurately that she was herself again, and they had a very much delayed breakfast from the food that Walter had put in James's pack before the trouble began.

"What will happen to him?" Lark asked anxiously. It seemed rather dreadful of them just to have left, with Walter still a prisoner.

"Nothing, I think," said James, who had been turning it over in his mind. "With me out of the picture, they haven't even a very good suspicion left, and those other customers were all really Roundheads as far as I know. Even if some of them were spies, they couldn't have seen or heard a thing that was suspicious. Of course, Walter will have to be especially careful for a while—" He stopped, realizing that he was saying far too much. He glanced anxiously at his small companion, busy braiding her hair, one corner of a pink tongue showing between her lips.

Lark looked back at him.

"I'm glad he'll be all right," she said artlessly. "People shouldn't be punished for just what they think, should they?"

James sighed in relief, and then looked at her sharply. He was beginning to wonder how a little girl could be so astonishingly astute in some things and so conveniently obtuse in others.

6
The Wood

On and on they trudged, sleeping in the open at night, well wrapped in cloaks. For this seemed safer than inns, and the nights were balmy and beautiful and glittering with stars. They heard no more about the two armies to the north, and James began to be more and more silent. His brown eyes were somber much of the time, and Lark, peering up at him, began to suspect quite accurately that he was finding her a burden. While he could not really bring himself to wish she had never been born, or even that he had not come to her rescue that day by the river bank, he did feel that she had timed her escapade very badly, that she was incredibly stubborn and he incredibly weak-willed, and that it was perfectly ridiculous for her to keep the upper hand this way. He glared at her.

Lark didn't miss the glare, and she had a very shrewd notion about what sort of thoughts caused it. She looked helpless and vulnerable with all her might, but James failed to notice. So she sighed and took the offensive again.

"James?" she asked in a small, thoughtful voice.

"Mm?" said James, engrossed in his dark thoughts.

"James, I was just wondering. What if I hadn't been at the Blue Dolphin that morning? I mean, what if you hadn't had a little sister crying and hanging around you when the Roundheads were going to carry you off?" She glanced at him sideways to see how he was responding to this, and noticed with satisfaction that he had got the point at once. He was really very quick-witted, in addition to being a hero, she decided, lowering her eyes demurely.

James began mentally kicking himself. It was true; she had saved his liberty if not his life, and he, monster of ingratitude, was busy wishing her a hundred miles away. And she must sense it, too, sensitive little creature that she was.

"Silly little Lark!" he jibed gently, warming her with his particularly sweet smile. "Of course, there may be some people who wouldn't consider my life worth saving, but since I'm very much attached to it—" He broke off, remembering that she should not know too much. "At least," he finished lamely, "you saved me a good bit of unpleasantness and delay at the very least, and I don't suppose I can ever tell you—" Once again he broke off, for there were too many things he could not say. He hoped she understood a little.

Lark, who understood very well the important fact that he had really been in considerable danger, stared down at the rumpled cloth of her skirt. It was a frightening thought that he might have been hanged or something. In addition it rather changed things. James became at once more precious and less godlike. He was not, after all, in full command of all situations, and now the dangers of their journey seemed a great deal more real.

James perceived her mood and seized the opportunity. "Now do you see what I mean, Lark? That was just a small incident compared to what it might have been if the sergeant hadn't been more reasonable than some Roundheads. And we still haven't run into any robbers or Gypsies, or a really tough soldier, or even a storm, or anything serious at all. Can't you see that it's quite mad to think of going to Scotland? By the way, where in Scotland were you intending to go, anyway?"

"Well, it's somewhere in Cameron country," Lark told him in a subdued voice.

"Cameron country!" James clutched his dark waving hair and rolled his eyes upward. "Cameron country!" he told the sky in despair. "Merciful heavens, send her a whole troop of guardian angels; one isn't nearly enough! My poor idiot Lark, do you know where Cameron country is? It's way up in the wilds of the Highlands! It's filled with the most terrifying steep and jagged mountains, such as you can't even begin to imagine, and wild savages, and clan wars, and raging torrents, and miles and miles of wilderness with no houses or people or roads. You can't do it, Lark. You can't begin to think of doing it. I wouldn't do it myself."

Lark looked at him with dismay. She had, up to now, been quite sure she would get her own way, and that James would do whatever mysterious business he had for the king, and then come to Scotland with her. Now the trip began to seem almost as impossible as he said it was. But she was *not* going back to Uncle Jeremiah's house! She stared mutinously at her own scuffed shoes.

James was encouraged by her silence. "Listen, Lark; I have an idea. I've some good friends in Shrewsbury. Now just wait a minute and listen to me! They'd be happy to have you stay with them for a while. *Do* keep quiet and let me finish, will you?"

Lark closed her mouth and listened, but not very encouragingly. James went on. "And then I have my own family in Devon."

Lark had her chin out. "That's nice," she said brightly.

"Now, stop that!" said James with annoyance. "Listen, I tell you! My family and friends in Devon are in touch with a good many of the exiles in France—the royal family, and a lot of the others. I'm sure they could get word of your parents, given a little time, and arrange to send you to them. But I can't take you to Devon myself, because I'm not going there, so I have to leave you some place where you'll be safe and where my father will be able to find you, and that's with my friends in Shrewsbury. Wouldn't you rather do that and get to your parents safely than to try to walk to Scotland alone?"

Lark considered. Her enthusiasm for Scotland had definitely waned. Perhaps . . . "Father's name isn't the same as Uncle Jeremiah's," she mused aloud. "So if I told you that, you still couldn't send me back to my uncle. And if it didn't work, I could still go to Scotland . . ."

James looked at her indignantly. "Don't you know me any better than that?" he demanded, hurt. "Lark, I want you to be happy almost as much as I want you to be safe. I know you'll be happiest with your family, so that's what I want for you. The only reason I'd even think of sending you back to your wicked uncle would be if that were the only way to keep you safe."

"Oh," said Lark in a small voice. She absorbed that for a moment and then smiled at him radiantly. Then he was fond of her!

In her delight at having this point cleared up, she felt that she must be fair to Uncle Jeremiah. "Actually," she confessed, "I suppose he isn't so very wicked; or at least he doesn't think he is. Even when he stole me from home, he thought he was doing the will of God. He has long conversations with God about everything, to be sure he's right. The only trouble is," she added astutely, "it always turns out that God agrees perfectly with Uncle Jeremiah, and when he prays out loud it's never asking God's opinion; it's just explaining to God what Uncle Jeremiah *thinks* He should do. I don't believe he can tell God's ideas apart from his own, you see."

She looked at James anxiously, hoping that he would understand this rather complicated idea, and also that he wouldn't notice that it was suspiciously complicated for the little girl that he supposed her to be.

But James was grinning appreciatively at her insight, no suspicions on his face. He had begun to take Lark's precocity for granted, particularly since he had no small sisters with which to compare her.

"I've noticed that a lot of Puritans can't tell their notions from God's," he observed wryly. "I think it's both their strength and their weakness. It's the thing that makes the good ones saints and the bad ones devils, and all of them dangerous because they lack a sense of humor."

"A sense of humor?" echoed Lark.

James nodded. "A real sense of humor is being able to laugh at yourself, and how can you do that if you take yourself so seriously that you think God depends on you for advice?"

It was a good thing he had been speaking quietly. They had hardly heard the soft clopping of a horse ambling along in the soft dust of the road behind them, and they were considerably startled when it loomed up alongside and a middle-aged man in Puritan garb leaned over and spoke.

"Good day," he said politely enough, but his dark eyes rested on Lark with what seemed unwarranted curiosity. "What is your name, little maid?"

Lark instantly donned the expression of a kitten who had just got its eyes open for the first time. She looked up. "My name is Submit Tanner," she piped, "and my brother is Humble Tanner, please, sir." Her fingers clutched for the protection of James's sleeve, and she ducked her head and twisted her feet in a most convincing agony of shyness. In any case, she had not the remotest idea of what to say or do next. Her inspiration had apparently used itself up for the day.

James took over. "Aye," he said in his best Yorkshire. "Tha mun pardon ma wee sister, for she do be main bashful, like, and not used to strangers. Mind tha manners, Submit," he added. Lark took the hint and bobbed a small curtsey, eyes still on the ground. "Did tha want summat?" James asked with ingenuous candor.

The man shook his head. "No," he said. "I stopped to ask about your sister because I heard the other day about a lost girl they're searching for down south of Salisbury. She has long brown hair, they say, and was wearing a brown dress and cloak when she disappeared—but there was no brother mentioned, and in any case, I believe the lost girl was rather older."

James hardly heard that last bit, because he was busy arranging his face into the proper expression. "Ah, th' poor lass!" he said with great sympathy. "Happen her folks'll be wild, just! Submit, tha mun say a prayer for her." He shook his head sadly. "Ah hopes them'll be finding her safe," he added. "Good day."

"Good day," said the man, and rode on.

James and Lark followed silently—but not too rapidly. The moment the man was out of sight ahead, they turned with perfect accord into a lane which led off the main road and through a wood. Better a little more delay than another encounter like that!

At first they proceeded fairly cheerfully, considering everything. For they were both greatly relieved at having the question of Scotland more or less settled, and the green shade was most welcome after the blazing heat of the road.

Soon a breeze sprang up from the west, but it wasn't welcome for long. It was a malicious breeze, tugging meanly at them, and blowing dust into their eyes. Lark soon found herself taking a personal dislike to it. James disliked it for rather more practical reasons. He very much feared that they were in for something more violent than a mere summer shower.

He began walking a little faster, even though they were both tired. For there were no signs of any house or shelter, and the sun, as it slipped down the northwest sky, was dimming behind a reddish gray haze. The breeze quickened until it was distinctly a wind, with a fretful whine to it. By sunset it was blowing leaves from the trees, and James and Lark were wrapped in their flapping cloaks, with heads lowered against the unpleasant weather.

It was quite dark, and the wind close to a gale, before James spied a light off to the left, just before a squall of rain blocked it out. "Come on, Lark," he urged, putting his arm around the small cloaked figure. "I see lights."

They lurched on through wind and rain, glimpsing brief flickers between the trees and lashing branches now and then. Presently they stood on the edge of a clearing looking at a group of lights within a larger group of dark shapes. James stared intently. "Gypsies," he announced.

Lark started to turn hastily away, as James had given her the impression only today that Gypsies were very much to be avoided. So, for that matter, had everyone who ever mentioned them. But James held her arm. "Wait," he said, his voice clear in a sudden brief lull of the wind.

Instantly several dogs from the Gypsy camp started barking excitedly. "Wait," said James again. "I've a blood friendship with one Gypsy. I don't suppose we could be lucky enough to have run into his tribe, but let's see what happens. Don't be afraid, Lark; they can be very warm and generous if they accept you at all."

Lark looked at him reproachfully, not sure whether he was fibbing a little bit now, or had been earlier. But she stood still, for she certainly had no intention of going off in the dark and storm without James.

7
The Gypsies

A cluster of lanterns glided toward them across the clearing, led by the still-barking dogs. Presently James and Lark were in a half-circle of feeble light, looking across a small but somehow uncrossable space at the Gypsies. Their swarthy faces had a golden sheen in the yellow light, and their once-bright garments seemed to glow softly: amethyst, russet, wine, and green. In the center was a massive, bearded man whose brows hung so far over his eyes that one could see only a deep shadow beneath, and beside him stood a woman whose age might be anywhere from thirty to sixty. Her faded crimson cloak hung to the ground in great wide folds, and her eyes were deep and black and penetrating. They regarded James and Lark silently, disconcertingly.

James spoke first. "My little sister and I are lost in the storm. May we beg shelter from you for the night?"

The woman reached a long arm from her cloak and pointed it almost at Lark's nose. "Why do you lie, young Gorgio? She is not your sister, nor is she a young child." The arm shot back in again, and the silence continued, more suspicious now.

Lark moved a little closer to James, alarmed at the obvious supernatural powers of the Gypsy woman. James spared a brief and interested glance at Lark. He already suspected that she was a trifle older than he had at first thought. Then he bestowed a frank and engaging grin upon the woman. "It's true that she is not my sister," he admitted cheerfully. "But since when do Gypsies object to a good lie?"

The atmosphere thawed a trifle, and the granite planes of the big man's face softened a tiny bit. "Yours was not a very good lie," he pointed out. "Sheba saw through it at once."

James bowed his head respectfully in Sheba's direction. "That's true, but she is clearly a woman of great wisdom. The Gorgios from whom we are in danger have been easily fooled so far."

The atmosphere thawed a little more. Gypsies were inclined to be sympathetic to anyone else who was also pursued by Gorgio authorities, and life had been particularly hard for them since the Puritans came to power in Britain. "Why are you in danger?" asked the man.

"It's a long story," James replied. "We will tell you the truth of it—but we are cold and wet. May we not come to one of your tents or wagons? Surely you need not fear that we could harm you, and you may cast us out any time you wish."

There was a silence, and James was suddenly sure that it was not the huge man who would really make the decision, but that they were all waiting some signal from the woman, Sheba. But Sheba had meanwhile pulled the crimson cloak away from her sides, like wings, to show Lark two small children standing under it like nestlings, one on each side. The younger one was like a small bird: round and chubby with rosy cheeks. The larger was clearly an imp of Satan, for wickedness danced in his black eyes, and he grinned at her in shy impudence.

Lark smiled delightedly and, afraid of alarming the small one, very gently moved one hand toward them a little. It was only then that she became aware of everyone watching, and she glanced up, startled.

Sheba moved her head slightly, swept the cloak around the children once again, and turned to lead the way back to the camp. The decision had been made.

A few minutes later James and Lark sat in one of the crowded wagons, in the midst of a whole family of Gypsies. Lanterns dangled, swaying slightly, from the roof, and their sodden cloaks hung at one end to drip. In weather like this there could be no campfires, but at least it was dry in the wagon, and warm with many bodies pressed closely together.

Still, there had been fires in the camp before the rain started, for Sheba brought them bowls of a strange, savory smelling stew with meats and vegetables and herbs cooked together. Lark looked at it a trifle dubiously, for she had never eaten anything like it, and vegetables were a bit of a novelty, in any case. But she was extremely hungry, so she had two bowls. And when she had finished, she decided that it had been delicious.

She looked around and began to perceive things that could not be seen. For one thing, although she and James were in the center of a crowded group, there was still that invisible wall between them and the others. For the Gypsies were a people apart. They might—rarely and under special conditions—give shelter to a couple of young Gorgios on a stormy night, but that didn't really change anything. Any non-Gypsy was a Gorgio, and Gorgios were alien creatures who could never enter the inner circle.

Lark began to feel uncomfortable. The faces around her were alien and mysterious. The big man, Psammis, was without doubt on very good terms with the Devil, and so was one of the younger men—a slender, straight, handsome fellow, with flashing eyes and too-white teeth under a black mustache. These people clearly knew and did things that Lark would prefer not even to imagine, though there was something to be liked about them, too. Sheba might almost have been a prophetess from the Old Testament. Her weather-beaten face was quite inscrutable, but her eyes gleamed with kindness as well as knowledge of things unknown.

The eating was finished now, and an air of waiting grew stronger. James looked around and began to speak, while Lark sat straighter. She nodded every so often as James told the story of their meeting and adventures, and now and then put in some little detail that he had forgotten. And when they had finished, she looked around at the sealed faces of their hosts, wondering what they were thinking.

"It is hard to believe that you do not know each other's names," pointed out the darkly handsome young man. "Do not you Gorgios trust one another?"

"I told you, it would not be safe for Lark to know my full name and my business," said James patiently. "It might endanger her."

Sheba nodded, but her deep eyes flickered briefly at Lark, who got the distinct impression that Sheba knew that Lark knew more than James thought she did. She shifted the subject hastily.

"I didn't trust James at first," she announced candidly, "because he was so worried about keeping me safe that he might have tried to take me back for my own good. But that's different from the other kind of not trusting."

It was Psammis who nodded this time. It seemed that they would be allowed to stay for the night.

But James had bigger ideas. "Do you know Frongo Lee, of the Blackbird tribe?" he asked suddenly.

Wary blankness covered every face, and Psammis looked at him. "What of Frongo Lee?" he asked.

"I have a blood friendship with him," announced James, and pulled up his left sleeve to show a thin scar along the inner side of his arm, with an oddly shaped extra little scar at the top of it. Psammis and Sheba examined it in silence.

"Tell," said Sheba, sitting back again and taking the sleepy younger child into her lap.

"It started by chance," said James, grinning ruefully. "About six months ago Frongo and I happened to get into a bit of trouble at the same time with the same troop of Roundhead soldiers—though for different reasons. Well, since 'the enemy of my enemy is my friend,' we helped each other out, and what with one thing and another we managed to get away after quite an interesting little fight. So naturally we mopped up each other's scratches once we were safe; and when we finished, we realized that we'd mingled blood anyhow, and saved each other's lives. So we just went ahead and made it official, and he added his little mark to the cut on my arm, and I helped him get back to his tribe, and then stayed on with them for a week or two. That was up in Lincolnshire," he added, and then cocked his head at them.

Psammis looked at the mark on his arm again, and then at James. "Well?"

"If you are going north soon, I would ask that we go with you for a way," said James bluntly. "No one would think to find us here, and we could wear Gypsy garments and stay in the wagons if necessary. Do you befriend the blood friends of your people that far?"

Lark was looking at him with enormous eyes. The Gypsies looked at each other. "We must talk about it," decided Psammis, after a long look at Sheba's face. "Sleep now. When you wake in the morning, we will let you know."

Lark must have been more tired than ever before in her life. She was finally awakened the next day by a stir and buzz from the camp around her, but mostly by something poking her. She opened her eyes. The wicked small imp she had first seen under Sheba's cloak sat with black eyes sparkling at her and his chubby small sister beside him. He wagged his head.

"Sheba said to let you sleep late because you were tired," he said, "but she could not have meant so *very* late. The sun is at the top of the sky, and we are setting out. Don't you want to wake up now?"

Lark blinked, yawned, and looked about her. There was no sign of James, nor did she hear his voice among the ones outside. She felt a moment of alarm, and then relaxed, knowing that he would take care of her, no matter what happened.

The young imp nudged her again. "Don't you want to get up?" he repeated. "There are some clothes here for you." He indicated a not-too-clean skirt of faded violet and a full-sleeved saffron blouse which lay by the pallet. "Your man has already changed, and we have to hide your Gorgio clothes with his. Hurry."

Lark sat up and looked at him with amused severity. "I can't change with a man in here with me, can I?" she demanded.

The imp looked flattered but puzzled. "Why not?"

Lark was saved the trouble of trying to explain by the arrival of a Gypsy girl whom she had just glimpsed among the group on the night before. The girl whirled into the wagon and let loose a flood of Romany speech at the boy, who answered with a cheeky grin. The older girl then cuffed his ear, pushed him bodily out of the wagon, and turned to Lark.

"That Bracken is a son of Satan," she announced. "If he gives you any trouble, beat him, or call me to do it." She looked pleased at the prospect. "Don't ever hit Berry, though," she added, nodding at the partridge-like child who squatted stolidly in the far corner, regarding them with solemn eyes and a mouth as small as a button. "She is our pet, and no one is allowed to hit her. I'm Willow, and I'll help you to change."

Lark, although a fairly strong-minded person herself,

was quite overwhelmed for the moment by the forcefulness of Willow. In any case, she was at a disadvantage, being still sleepy and confused by her strange surroundings. It would be best to submit and then find James as soon as possible.

She studied Willow from the corner of her eyes as the girl helped her out of the crumpled brown dress and into the more crumpled violet skirt. She was, to be honest, beautiful—at least if one liked tawny smooth skin, luxurious black hair curling over back and shoulders, and black eyebrows like wings in a narrow, lovely boned face. She must be about sixteen, Lark decided, and for some reason she was not altogether sure she was going to like her.

This was odd, for Willow was disarmingly friendly. She pulled and tugged at the blouse, and tied a scarlet sash around Lark's waist, being sure that it was artistically draped. And she exclaimed over the length and fineness of Lark's hair, unbraiding it for a better look.

"But it could never look like Gypsy hair," she decided, with a toss of her own. "Too straight and smooth and light. I could cut it, of course. No? Well, then, we will tangle the front a little and put a scarf over the rest." She did so, while Berry went on watching from her corner like a small sphinx, and Bracken called an occasional insult from outside the wagon.

"Psammis says you and the young man may walk with us except on roads where Gorgios travel," said Willow when she was satisfied with Lark's appearance. She gave Lark a sideways look. "He is very beautiful, this young man you travel with. Is he yours? If you don't even know his name, you can't know him *very* well. I think I like him." And grabbing Berry around her plump middle, she heaved her from the wagon and vanished around the side, Berry kicking and roaring at being torn from her new interest.

Lark frowned as she climbed down from the wagon. Now she knew why she didn't much care for Willow. But she didn't put it into words, even to herself.

Around the corner of the wagon was a busy scene. Thick blanket tents were being taken from the bent hazel sticks which had held them up, and all sorts of items were being piled into the gaily painted wagons. James came around the other end of the one where Lark had slept, gave her a casual glance, and then jumped and looked again.

"I didn't know you!" he said.

He didn't look much like himself, either, in colorful breeches and shirt of blue and faded crimson, and Lark said so, with spirit and a touch of tartness which surprised James.

"Don't you want to travel with the Gypies for a bit?" he asked. "Really, Lark, it's much the safest thing we could do."

She nodded agreement, and he looked at her again, wondering what was wrong. "Psammis says we had better stay apart," he went on. "Two Gorgios together might attract attention where one wouldn't. I'm to walk among the grown-ups, and you're to stay with the children. That's all right, isn't it?"

"Oh, just fine!" snapped Lark. "I'm sure Berry and Bracken and I will get along simply splendidly!"

8

Willow

She knew it! Craning her head, Lark could see Willow's unmistakable green dress and black head walking outrageously close to James up ahead. Lark didn't even hear Bracken's running chatter of uncomplimentary remarks—much to that cheeky lad's annoyance. She kept glaring ahead blackly until Willow threw a triumphant glance over her shoulder and moved even closer to James.

Lark set her teeth. Pride arose in her. Turning to Bracken, she flashed him a smile that caused him to blink and decide that there was perhaps more to some Gorgio girls than met the eye, and just possibly he would not put gorse and nettles in her bed quite yet, after all.

"Is Willow your sister, Bracken?" asked Lark.

Bracken made an extremely rude noise which Lark interpreted as yes. She looked at him, not without sympathy. "Don't you like her?" she asked disarmingly.

"I hate her!" Bracken announced with all the earnestness of a small boy talking about his older sister. "I wish she would hurry and get married, so that instead of her beating me, she would have a husband to beat her. When I get big enough, I shall beat her every day, myself."

Carried away by the prospect, he turned a somersault which hurtled him into the middle of the group of children in front. The entire group immediately turned into a violent battle. But before Lark had a chance to worry lest they might all be attacking Bracken at once, she saw that it was everyone against everyone else. Each child happily clawed, kicked, pummeled, and bit whoever was in reach. None of the grown-ups paid any attention at all until the fracas threatened to hold up the wagon behind. Then the darkly handsome man with the black mustache came forward, waded into the battle, and began kicking and tossing children out into the meadow off the path with cheerful impartiality. After the road was cleared, he wandered back to his own place, while the children picked themselves up with no apparent damage or resentment whatever, and went back to their places in the procession.

Bracken swaggered back to Lark with several more rips in his tattered shirt, a swelling lip, and the air of a conquerer. "I won that one, didn't I?" he bragged.

"Did you?" asked Lark dubiously. It hadn't seemed evident.

"Of course I did. If I hadn't been winning, Neco would never have bothered to come rescue the others."

Lark had her doubts about this, but she kept them to herself. "Is Neco your brother?" she asked, thinking that they were a great deal alike—both being swaggering, and wicked-eyed, and rather charming in a satanic way.

Bracken hooted at the idea. "No, dolt, he is the grandson of the brother of my mother's mother, and also the son of the sister of the wife of the brother of my father." Lark was silent for a moment, trying with very little success to sort out this complicated family tree. "He is the one," added Bracken, cocking his black, bullet-shaped head at her, "whom I hope will marry Willow, for he will beat her more often than any of the other young men in the tribe."

Lark, having caught another glimpse of the two heads up in front, was inclined to think this a very good idea. "Does he want to marry her?" she asked hopefully.

"Oh, yes, and I think she wants to marry him. But not yet. She is a wicked flirt, Willow is, and she is having a great deal of fun making eyes and wiggling her hips at all the other young men—especially other girls' young men," he added with a knowing sidelong glance at Lark. "She is flirting with your young man this very minute," he informed her with glee.

Lark indicated elaborately that she could not possibly care, and although Bracken might not have believed her altogether, he seemed much impressed by her careless attitude. It even occurred to him that it was a pity she was a Gorgio.

For the rest of the day Lark chatted with Bracken and turned over a new idea in the back of her mind. She wondered how one went about flirting, and if she would be any good at it. For the first time, it occurred to her that a childish appearance might on some occasions be a distinct disadvantage. She still hadn't made up her mind when they stopped to make camp . . . but another glimpse of Willow clinging to James's arm helped.

For a while things looked better, while camp was being set up. James helped with the tents, proving quite experienced at bending and fastening the hazel rods, and pinning the coarse brown blankets over them with the long thorns of wild sloe. Willow, meanwhile, was captured by Sheba and put to work helping cook the meal. But Lark, feeling very inadequate, joined the children in fetching water and firewood. And Sheba gave her a knowing, mischievous look as if to say, "If you will play the role of a child, then you must stay with the children."

When the tribe sat down around the campfire to eat, there was Willow again, close against James's side, even feeding him choice bits from her own plate. James, to do him justice, did have the grace to look highly uncomfortable, and to refuse her offerings as politely as possible. But Lark told herself angrily that if he had any strength of will whatever, he could do more than that—unless, of course he *liked* it! She stared at him intently. It was true that there did not seem to be any romance in the way he behaved toward Willow—but on the other hand, there was even less in the way he behaved toward Lark. At least he saw Willow as a young lady and not a mere child!

Willow at that point threw Lark another glance of laughing triumph. *She* had a shrewd idea of Lark's true age, reflected Lark in exasperation, even if that noddle-skulled James didn't. She smiled back at Willow benignly, and spent the rest of the meal studying the Gypsy girl's technique.

At the end of the meal, Lark's opportunity came. Neco strolled by and paused near her, still looking like Satan in a handsome disguise. Lark took a deep breath, and then gave him one swift melting glance from the corners of her eyes, up through her lashes, just as Willow had done with James.

Neco seemed for an instant not to take it in. Then he blinked and turned his full attention to the little Gorgio. He perceived at once that Sheba had been right in saying that she was no child. He also perceived that she was a charming little thing, and it occurred to him that this might be a splendid opportunity to teach that shameless flirt of a Willow a good lesson. It did not occur to him—for he was a conceited young man—that Lark might be doing exactly the same thing.

He smiled down at her, his white teeth flashing under the small black mustache, and his dark cheeks creasing. He sat down. "I have not yet been properly introduced to our charming young Gorgio guest," he remarked. "My name is Neco; what is yours?"

Lark told him, half alarmed at the success of her plot, and not at all sure what to say or do next. To Neco, her confusion made her all the more delightful. He decided he was going to enjoy the process of punishing Willow.

James, across the campfire, was still patiently enduring the attentions of the Gypsy girl, which were becoming not only uncomfortable, but distinctly embarrassing. Moreover, he was aware of the hidden amusement of the other Gypsies. And yet, what could he do? Willow did not seem to take a hint at all well, and he didn't want to do anything that might really offend her or her family. After all, he *was* their guest. She practically had her head on his shoulder by now, and he groaned mentally.

He was also beginning to feel a certain amount of

pique at Lark. Why didn't she come to his rescue? Her refreshing small self at this point would have made things much less awkward. But she didn't seem interested in James's company any more. She had scarcely spoken to him all day. Instead, she seemed perfectly happy with the company of that demonic little boy.

James glanced broodingly across the campfire, and suddenly jerked upright. The demonic little boy had been exchanged for an even more demonic young man, who was being a great deal too attentive to Lark—especially considering her tender years! For an instant, James found himself wondering once again just exactly how tender her years *were*—but that wasn't the point. She was *much* too young for Neco to be flirting with. Besides, James discovered that he had mistrusted Neco from the very beginning, and now positively loathed him.

Lark chose that moment to give Neco an uncertain but quite enchanting smile. Neco smiled back possessively. James clenched his teeth and drew in his breath sharply.

Willow looked up to see what was wrong with James, and then she in turn stiffened to outraged attention. She glared across the fire. All conversation stopped for a moment, as the others surveyed the situation with considerable interest and waited to see what would happen next. Neco looked up and grinned fiendishly at Willow, while Lark managed to look brightly innocent.

Willow was not a girl to give up easily. Inspired by the unexpected competition, she wove her slim arms around James's neck and definitely placed her curly black head on his chest.

With a muffled "Excuse me!" James abruptly detached

the clinging hands, stood up, and strode out of the camp circle into the dark stretch of meadow behind.

A ripple of amusement went through the circle of Gypsies, who seemed to feel that Willow was getting what was coming to her. And Willow, doubly humiliated, sent a poisonous look after James. Lark stared after him, too, but with dismay. She had already begun to wonder if she had bitten off more than she could chew. Neco was threatening to get quite out of hand, and she had been fighting down rising panic with the certainty that James would surely come to her rescue. Now James was gone, and Neco's tender words and melting eyes were distinctly unnerving. Lark had never felt so alone in her life.

She hadn't time to feel that way long. With a furious hiss, Willow strode across to Lark and Neco and loosed a torrent of Romany that didn't really need any translation. Then, quick as a snake, she jerked off Lark's head scarf, flung it on the ground, and pulled her hair fiercely.

Lark squeaked with pain and surprise, and Neco's hands shot out. One of them seized Willow's wrist and the other gave her a resounding slap across the cheek. Bracken suddenly appeared on the scene, jumping up and down and shouting encouragement to Neco until Psammis reached out a massive hand of his own and tumbled the little boy to the ground. In any case, Neco seemed not to need any encouragement. With a perfectly diabolic smile he stood up, tucked Willow neatly under his arm, and strode out of the camp circle in the opposite direction to that which James had taken.

James had heard Lark's cry from his solitude in the dark, and now came rushing back prepared to defend her with his life. He arrived just in time to see Neco exit with Willow, and he paused at the edge of the group, confused. Things were going on which he did not altogether understand. Lark seemed to be safe, after all.

While he hesitated, there came from the darkness nearby a series of thumps, of the kind which might easily have been made by a hazel wand, say, beating against the thickness of full skirts. These were accompanied by a series of shrill yelps. James blinked, but no one seemed to be paying much attention except Lark and Bracken, who looked at each other with great satisfaction.

"Now he will marry her at once," said Bracken, pleased. "And you," he added generously, "can have your Gorgio man."

Lark blushed hotly and hoped James hadn't heard. She also wished he would come and sit by her. Was he no longer even interested in being friends? Or was he so angry that he would never forgive her?

But James was not angry at all. On the contrary, he was no longer sure of anything concerning Lark—not even his own feelings, which seemed to be rather more complicated than he had thought. He looked at her. She was chatting with Bracken, not even looking his way. He could not just go on standing there. Diffidently he made his way through the small crowd of Gypsies, who were now laughing and talking just as if nothing had happened, and took the place beside Lark which Neco had left empty.

Just then Willow and Neco reappeared, looking flushed and very much pleased with themselves. "I have beat her soundly, and now we are going to be married," announced Neco masterfully, once in Romany and again in English for the benefit of the Gorgio guests. "There will be no flirting from Willow—except with me, of course."

Lark noticed that he didn't say a thing about whether *he* would flirt or not, but Willow seemed not to notice this omission. She let Neco lead her back to where she and James had been sitting, looking quite lovely and radiant, and Lark found that she did not really hate her, after all. Even Neco seemed much less wicked—especially from across a blazing bonfire with his newly betrothed occupying all his attention. She smiled happily.

James noticed that she seemed to be perfectly delighted at this betrothal of Willow and Neco, and he breathed more easily. He must have mistaken her expression earlier when he thought she was trying to flirt with Neco. He watched the pure line of her throat and cheek outlined by the firelight, transparently young and innocent and vulnerable. A mere child after all, he told himself firmly and with a sense of great relief—for with one thing and another, he felt his life was quite complicated enough for the moment as it was.

Leaning forward, he put his mouth very close to Lark's small ear. "What a minx that Willow is!" he murmured. "I think she and Neco suit each other splendidly, and I hope they'll keep each other very busy from now on."

Lark turned a demure but impish eye upon him. "So do I," she agreed. And James never suspected just how thoroughly she meant it.

9
Doll

Lark would have been happy to remain a Gypsy for a very long time. The freedom of such things as bare feet and doing very much what one liked was almost unbelievable after two years in a Puritan household. Still, she did see that even freedom could be carried too far. For instance, she could not really approve the Gypsy habit—almost a fine art—of acquiring things that did not belong to them.

But one cloudy day, just a few miles from Shrewsbury, this pleasant and casual way of life ended.

The caravan stopped, quite unexpectedly, and Lark, peering ahead, could see Psammis and Sheba staring at the ground.

"A pataran!" squeaked Bracken, darting forward. Lark stayed there, remembering vaguely that James had told her that a pataran was a special arrangement of rocks, twigs, and leaves which was a whole message to a Gypsy, but that no one else would even notice at all.

Presently Bracken was back, rubbing his shabby green breeches where he had been smacked for being in the way, but as irrepressible as ever. "It says to be cautious," he announced gleefully. "There may be danger ahead."

Lark's eyes immediately searched the gathering Gypsies for James. "What will we do now?" she asked Bracken.

Bracken shrugged. "Oh, we will just send someone ahead to find out what the danger is, and come back and tell us."

Sure enough, Neco and another man set off ahead of the caravan, and when they returned, the Gypsies had a conference in the field beside the river. James and Lark tactfully waited by themselves behind the yellow wagon, James more uneasy than he liked to admit. Then Sheba and Psammis came over to them.

"An army of Scots is headed this way from Chester," said Psammis. "It is said that General Cromwell and an even larger army is following them, and when they catch up there will surely be a great battle. This is no place for us, and we will turn and go into Wales, perhaps, or to the east. What of you? Will you stay with us?"

James's lips tightened as he considered this. But he really had no choice. "Thank you," he said, "but I must go on to Shrewsbury." And he smiled a little wryly at Lark, hoping he wasn't leading her straight into a battle instead of to the safety of his friends.

Lark, who would have followed him into a fiery furnace, smiled back trustfully, and they both turned into their respective wagon homes to change back into Puritan clothing.

The tribe gathered to wish them well and put some

good-luck spells upon them. Bracken complained bitterly about losing his new playmate, and Neco winked at Lark wickedly and then had to grab the enraged Willow's wrists. James thanked Psammis and Sheba as if they had been royalty—which, among their own people, they were, in a way.

"If I can ever repay you—" he began.

"You are our friend, Friend of Frondo," said Psammis sonorously. "Let you repay by helping another Gypsy in trouble if you can, no matter if he has broken every law in England—which," he added with a chuckle, "will probably be the case."

"I won't even stop to ask," promised James.

As they started to walk away, Lark saw the stolid small figure of Berry, still hunched sphinx-like in the back of the yellow wagon, regarding them solemnly. It occurred to her that she had not yet heard the child speak a word. Impulsively she called "Goodbye, Berry," and waved.

Berry considered her for a moment, her mouth pulled into a mere button of pink. Then, just as Lark had given up, she raised a chubby brown hand and gravely wiggled the short fingers—exactly twice. Then she relapsed once more into a statue of a child. Lark grinned.

They walked along toward the hill town of Shrewsbury, their feet feeling very strange in shoes. James was silent, and it was clear that his thoughts were not particularly pleasant. Lark watched him anxiously from under her long lashes.

"James," she ventured at last, "do you think Psammis was right about the armies and Cromwell?"

"Probably," said James gloomily.

"And there is going to be a big battle soon?"

"I shouldn't be surprised," said James, even more gloomily.

Lark peered at him sideways. "You're afraid the Roundheads will win, aren't you?"

James nodded, and Lark was plunged instantly into depression. For James was extremely wise, and if he thought Cromwell would win, then it would probably happen. James saw her face and tried to cheer her up. "Perhaps not," he added, not very convincingly.

"Would it be my fault if it happens?" asked Lark in a very small voice, and James stared at her with astonishment.

"How could it be your fault?" he demanded.

"I mean, if I'm the one who delayed you, and something bad happened because you weren't in time to do whatever it is you have to do," explained Lark disconsolately.

James frowned. "What do you mean?" he asked severely.

Lark turned appealing round eyes to his. "I'm awfully sorry," she pleaded, "but I can't help knowing. I tried not to, but you can't un-know a thing if you know it."

With a rueful sigh, James realized that he really shouldn't have expected her not to guess something. "Well," he asked gently, "what is it that you do know, Lark?"

"Not very much," said Lark, relieved that he wasn't angry. "Only I know you're doing something for the king, and I think you're supposed to do it in Shrewsbury, and you're worried for fear you'll be too late. And if something awful happened because I made you late, I just couldn't bear it."

James experienced a wave of tenderness as he looked down at her—brave and loyal little comrade that she was! "If it hadn't been for you, back at the Blue Dolphin, I might not have got here at all," he pointed out logically. "So you see, you've been far more a help than a handicap. Anyway," he added a little wryly, "what I'm doing isn't in the least all that important. In fact, I dare say I shan't be of any use now, at all, with the armies this far south. But you see, I said I'd be there, so I must. There may be some message I can still take somewhere—or something."

Lark sighed with relief and closed her mouth firmly so as not to ask any more questions that she shouldn't. James smiled down at her. "It isn't that I don't trust you, because I do," he said. "It's partly for your own safety that I don't tell you more, and partly because these aren't my secrets to tell."

James trusted her! Lark sighed and cherished the words all the rest of the way to Shrewsbury.

Shrewsbury was a walled town on a hill, with a castle at the main gate that was clearly occupied by Roundhead soldiers. Lark breathed deeply, ducked her head like a shy child, and clung to James as they walked through the gate and up the steep curve of the cobbled street.

At the top of the hill, James turned to the left with an air of knowing exactly where he was going, and led the way to a fine, high, timbered inn with casement windows in front jutting over an oaken balcony. Above the balcony swung a sign which proclaimed it the Word-of-God Inn, but it seemed clear that this name was a fairly recent afterthought. For in front of the balcony swung a fine big dragon, beautifully carved, and painted a now-faded but impressive red. At least Lark thought it was a dragon, although it might possibly have been a griffin. At any rate, its claws were lifted fiercely and there was a most ferocious fanged head at the end of the long curved neck.

"Doll's husband was a frightfully stern Puritan when he was alive," murmured James, who noticed Lark staring at the dragon. "So everyone assumes that Doll feels the same way. But she has always been secretly on the Royalist side, and it's very useful, especially with the inn's reputation. It's the last place anyone would suspect."

He opened the heavy door and led the way in, finding his way directly down the long hallway and to another door, out of which came a glow of light and the murmur of voices. Lark stared in past the leanness of James. It was the kitchen, heart and core of this inn, where food was cooked, and people not wealthy enough to dine privately upstairs sat around and ate.

It was a huge room, with a scrubbed table in the center of the stone-flagged floor. There were pewter mugs and blue-and-white plates set for supper, and several men sitting in high-backed settees along the wall and on both sides of the enormous stone arch which held the fireplace. The fire blazed cheerfully on the raised stone hearth; and on racks above and on both sides hung long steel spits, brass skimmers and ladles, skillets, pans, and tongs. The mantel shelf was a neat clutter of candle stands, skewers, pewter plates, salt box, tinder box, and even flour dredgers and smoothing irons. Lark reflected that both James's and her collars, though freshly washed just a day ago in a stream, could stand a touch of the smoothing iron.

The five or six men, all in Puritan dress, glanced up more or less casually at the new guests, and an extremely plump woman—apparently the cook—turned from her task of frying bacon in a large shallow pan. Her round cheeks glowed with the warmth of the fire, and no one could have imagined a more good-natured, motherly, simple-hearted sort of creature.

"New guests," she called. "Come in, m'dears, come in."

But James was busy playing his role. He looked around dubiously and spoke up with his old Yorkshire voice. "Be this a gradely and godly inn where happen ah can bring ma wee sister?"

"Bless your heart, it is that!" exclaimed the cook, turning the bacon over to the chambermaid and coming toward them. "As fine as you'll find in the whole of Shropshire, and none staying here but fine godly folk who will never offend her innocent ears with an untoward word. Sit down, sit down, and supper will be ready soon."

She turned back to her work—but not before Lark had caught an unmistakable *look* between her and James. So this, then, was Doll, and surely no one ever looked less capable of playing a double role! Lark relaxed and enjoyed her meal.

It was not too long after supper that the guests began drifting out, bound for the large common room which held a number of beds for those who could not afford private rooms. Doll kept bustling around with fussy kindness and chitter-chatter as long as any of the other guests were still there. James, she announced, could have a pallet here in the kitchen where it was warm, nice lad that he was, and his sweet sister would sleep snugly and safely up with Doll in her own bedroom, so she should.

But the instant the last guest left the kitchen, Doll became brisk and businesslike. She even looked, suddenly, less plump than solid as she turned and studied James severely. "Who's the child?" she demanded, jerking her chin at Lark. "This isn't a game we're playing, James Trelawney!"

Her voice was low, even though they were in the arched section, close by the fireplace, and no one could have heard from outside. But low though her voice was, it was sharp. Lark flushed and dropped her chin, and made a mental note of James's last name. It was nice. Trelawney. Lark Trelawney would sound well, too.

James's chin jerked upward. "She's to be trusted," he said curtly. "In fact, it was her wits got me out of a very nasty mess. Don't think you can judge people by their size or age, Doll!"

Doll turned and looked hard at Lark, who felt that she had to defend James's judgment. "Anyhow, he hasn't told me anything," she pleaded. "I didn't even know his last name until you said it just now, and he doesn't know mine, either. We only know we're both on the same side . . . but I expect I'd better go to bed or something now, so you can talk," she added humbly.

Doll went on staring at her for a moment longer, and Lark was surprised all over again at how different she looked now. Then the massive shoulders shrugged. "Well, I suppose it's no matter now, anyway," she observed, turning back to James. "There's no need any longer for the kind of work you've been doing. It's not messengers will be needed now, but soldiers."

Lark didn't hear any more, because something located somewhere under her ribs began behaving most alarmingly. She felt choked and blind and deaf, and altogether dreadful, and she had a sudden long-ago memory of how very odd and still her mother's face had been when Father went off to the wars.

James leaped to his feet. "Lark, are you ill?" he demanded in a great worry. "Did I make you walk too far? You should have told me if you didn't feel up to it; there wasn't all *that* much hurry!" Doll looked extremely disapproving of that last statement, but James didn't notice. "Doll, *do* something, please! You can see she isn't feeling well."

"Nonsense!" Doll put a broad hand on Lark's forehead. "Not a trace of fever, so it can't be serious. Stop fussing, James!" And she hustled the unprotesting Lark upstairs to her own chamber and a small pallet in the far corner, tucked her in, and told her to go right to sleep.

Lark nodded meekly, and then proceeded to lie awake for hours, seeing James being killed or wounded on a battlefield. For the first time in her life, she wished that King Charles II would go a long way away and never come back again.

10
The Quarrel

Lark awoke in the morning and stared at the unfamiliar ceiling for a moment, knowing vaguely that there was misery ready to pounce as soon as she remembered where she was. She tried not to think at all, but of course that just made her remember, after all, and the misery pounced.

James was going off to get himself killed in battle!

She looked around. Doll's bed was empty, and the gray light from the casement showed that it was well after dawn. She got up and dressed, thinking wretchedly about James. How like a man, she decided crossly. They would drop anything to go off and fight. And fighting, Lark suddenly discovered with great clarity, was the silliest thing ever invented! It never changed anyone's mind at all; and it didn't in the least prove who was right, but merely who was stronger; and all it did do was to kill people and make things worse than they were before the fighting started.

There had been fighting in England ever since Lark could remember. Father had been lamed, and Uncle Robert and two cousins killed, and her family driven from their home, and Lark herself snatched from her family. All of this had been part of life, and she had never very much questioned it, because it was the way things were. Now she began to ask if it was the way things *should* be, and it took her no time at all to decide that it wasn't. And if this was the way men insisted on running things, then Uncle Jeremiah must be quite wrong about masculine superiority, and perhaps women should take over for a while.

By the time she had got this far, a little awed by her own daring, she had also finished dressing and gone down the steep stairs. She entered the warm kitchen in a state of indignation which helped to blot out her misery, and she looked around. The room was empty except for a merry fire and Doll, who was cleaning up and scrubbing tables.

"Where's James?" demanded Lark, standing still.

Doll looked at the small sour face, and it was amazing how even her three chins seemed made of hard muscle rather than soft and gentle fat. "He's across town somewhere looking for a friend," said Doll. "There's food keeping warm on the shelf in the fireplace."

Lark wasn't very hungry, but Doll's firmness caused her to walk over and fill a plate with bread and butter and bacon. She sat down at the nearest table and fiddled with it. Doll finished scrubbing one table and moved to another. "Do you know what leeches are?" she asked suddenly.

Lark blinked. Indeed she knew what leeches were.

Horrid black slug-like things that clung to a person and sucked his blood. Doctors sometimes used them if they felt that a patient had an excess of blood in some spot or other.

"Do you?" persisted Doll.

Lark frowned. "Yes," she said darkly. "Nasty things."

"Nasty clinging things that suck the strength out of a man," added Doll. "Don't you be one, girl." She turned back to her scrubbing with an air of inviting Lark to think it over.

Lark stared at the broad back resentfully and declined the invitation. She knew without even a second thought that she did not care for the implications and she was not going to have anything to do with them. She pushed her plate away, partly because she didn't even want to eat Doll's food.

"Best eat up," advised Doll, going back to the hearth and beginning to polish copper pans. "I want you to help me. My chambermaid's run away home, scared of a battle, and if you're going to stay with me, you might as well be useful."

Lark had no intention of staying with her, but she did not say so. She picked up a piece of bread and nibbled. "When will James be back?"

"When he's ready," said Doll curtly. "You don't own him, you know. Come along, now, if you've finished, and lend a hand."

Lark obeyed sullenly, feeling that she had been tricked. She had thought James was going to introduce her to *nice* people—or better still, stay with her himself.

"You can go up and dust and straighten the private

rooms," Doll told her. "Here's a cloth. We've not many guests these days, what with two armies heading this way. You can assume that anyone staying here is a Parliament officer or sympathizer, and act accordingly."

Lark sniffed indignantly as she took the cloth. A person would think her a mere babe who had never fooled a Roundhead in her life! She stalked from the room, deciding that when women began running matters, Doll should not be allowed to help. She never did learn that Doll had heard all about her from James that morning, and was paying her a high compliment in trusting her into Roundhead chambers at all.

Upstairs Lark worked doggedly but with such vigor that it was a mercy there was nothing fragile around, or she would certainly have broken it. How quickly things could change! Yesterday there had been a happy if rather vague future ahead in which she and James would live happily ever after. It had never even faintly occurred to her that he might go off to war.

Lark snuffled and rubbed the back of her hand across her face, leaving a smudge. She had never doubted that she and James belonged to each other, for always and always. To be sure, he was not fully aware of this yet, because his mind was occupied with urgent matters, and because he thought of Lark as just a little girl. But he would come round to it. Already Lark had noticed that she seemed to be getting a little older in his thoughts, and she had decided that by her fourteenth birthday—which was an impressive age—he would be seeing her altogether as a Young Lady.

Blinking, she dusted the same side of the room all over

again, thinking of her dream. It was such a beautiful dream! It showed James as the Captain of their ship, which was Life, of course, always knowing what to do, and explaining things, and steering the ship ever so skillfully—with Lark watching and admiring and helping, and every now and again just giving the tiller a quiet little nudge when James wasn't particularly noticing, in order to be sure he was steering the ship where she wanted to go.

She finished dusting the last casement, opened it a crack, and stuck her face into the fine drizzle outside to cool it. She was beginning to feel very angry at James. He had let her think they were going to do everything she wanted—or very nearly—and that he was fond of her. But apparently he was even fonder of King Charles. Lark was even angrier at King Charles than she was at James. He had been very nice and kind years ago when he was just gangling, long-faced Prince Charles who came to see them and tease her sister and get into mischief with her brother. Apparently he had changed for the worse since those days.

The door behind her opened. Lark stood perfectly still except for waving her dust cloth a little, just in case it was a Roundhead, who might wonder what she was doing there. But she knew it wasn't a Roundhead. It was James. There was a certain feeling in the air when James was near.

"Lark?" said James anxiously.

Lark turned around with her back against the edge of the casement and looked at him pathetically. Her eyes were very round and shadowed, and James felt guilty and responsible.

"Are you still feeling ill, Lark?" he asked. "You shouldn't try to work if you are. Lark, I've been looking for the friends in Shrewsbury who were going to take you to mother and father, remember? Or at least I was going to ask them, but they aren't here."

"Then they can't take me," concluded Lark hopefully.

James shook his head. "But I do think you'll be perfectly safe here with Doll, and—"

"No!" Lark stamped her foot. "I won't! I won't stay here!"

"But Lark," exclaimed the bewildered James. "You agreed—"

"I did not!" Lark snapped. "I didn't say I'd stay with Doll; I hate her! And you didn't say a single word about going off to battle and getting yourself killed, or I wouldn't have agreed to anything!"

She stopped and turned her back on him, for a sudden intuition had warned her that this was the wrong sort of thing to say. One didn't ask men not to go off into danger, because the silly geese would then decide that this was the very thing they absolutely had to do, in order to prove their courage or something. But it was very difficult to think of any other arguments.

"That wasn't what we agreed at all," she muttered finally.

James stared at her obdurate back, greatly astonished. He didn't know what was wrong with her. His sweet and reasonable Lark was suddenly being about as sweetly reasonable as a dog fight. Come to think about it, *was* Lark such a sweetly reasonable child? James thought about it for a second or two, and concluded that she was not. At least, she was not when anything opposed her quiet determination to have her own way. Then she usually became sweetly *un*reasonable, and the reason she was now being so horrid was that for once being sweetly unreasonable had not worked.

James looked at her with less affection than he had ever felt for her, and wondered rather darkly how much the redoubtable grandmother had contributed to Lark's personality.

"What is the matter with you, Lark?" he demanded with considerable annoyance. Then he stifled his annoyance and tried to remember her extreme youth and make allowances. "Surely you understand that I want to do the best thing I can for you—but I have my loyalty to the King, don't forget. We both do."

Lark made a rude sound into the casement, but so faintly that James took it for the beginnings of sense, and was encouraged.

"You know I wouldn't choose to leave you behind," he went on earnestly but—at the moment—not altogether truthfully. "It's a matter of honor, Lark. Did you ever read the poem of Richard Lovelace that came out just a couple of years ago? He's a Royalist poet, you know, and the poem is called 'To Lucasta: Going to the Wars'; and the last lines go, 'I could not love thee, dear, so much, lov'd I not honor more.' Don't you think that's true of good friends like us, too?" He paused, looking very fatherly and feeling that he had put his case very well indeed.

"Fffft!" said Lark loudly, and this time the rudeness was unmistakable.

James gaped, and then reddened. He heroically restrained himself from boxing her ears. "You're behaving like a baby," he said coldly.

Lark whirled around to confront him with fury. There was something in his last remark that stung very deeply, and her cheeks turned pink and her round chin quivered with outrage. "You!" she cried. "You! You're acting like a baby yourself! You're worse; you're acting just like a *man!*"

James blinked. Those last words should have been a compliment, but the tone made it very clear that they were not.

"You think you're so clever and reasonable," fumed Lark, getting into the spirit of the thing. "You talk about being scientific and logical, and then you turn around and start being perfectly stupid, and you haven't even got enough sense to notice it!"

"What are you talking about?" demanded James, affronted by this slight to his intelligence.

"You said yourself that those Scots—the Covenanters that have the King—are even worse than the English Roundheads," said Lark, jutting her chin out at him. "You did; I heard you. And you said that they make King Charles do what they say, and that they want to rule England instead of Cromwell doing it, only they'll be even worse—and now you're all ready to go help them do it just because they have the King. And if they win things will be worse than ever, and you'll probably be dead besides, and I think you're being perfectly stupid!"

She stopped, a little astonished at herself. She hadn't really known that she thought those things before she heard herself saying them, but she was rather pleased with how much sense it made.

James stared at her in a kind of horror. This was an aspect of matters that he had never allowed himself to notice, and now that Lark had dragged it out and waved it in front of him, he simply didn't feel that he could cope with it at all. This was not surprising, for older and wiser men than he were finding it too much for them. Where *did* Royalist loyalty lie in all of this tangle?

James pushed the impossible question aside and proceeded to behave like a normal human being by turning all of his distress into anger, and then directing the anger toward the person who brought the whole thing to his attention.

"I'm afraid," he observed bitingly, "that you have lived too long with the Roundheads, Lark. Or perhaps you're just too young to have any notion of loyalty, although I should have *thought* your grandmother or someone would have taught it to you. Never mind, perhaps it's just as well. I expect you'll get along, no matter who wins. But in the meantime, I'm afraid you'll just have to stay with Doll for a while whether you like it or not, because there isn't any other place for you to go . . . unless, of course, you ask the Roundhead garrison at the castle to take care of you."

Lark, so terribly hurt by this that she really felt about to die of heartbreak, somehow kept her eyes dry and her chin up. "Oh, yes there is!" she retorted. "I can go to my sister in Scotland. And I don't need you, either." She stalked to the door, and just as she reached it, turned for one last word.

"I hope," she said distinctly, "that when Lucasta read that poem she slapped Mr. Lovelace's face for him."

She was gone, leaving James in a state of shock. Lark's inescapable logic rang in his ears, and he was not a person who could ignore such a question once he was aware of it. If he fought for King Charles, he was helping a worse tyranny than Cromwell—but what other choice did he have? He certainly couldn't help Cromwell against his king. And he couldn't just ignore the whole thing.

He put his face in his hands, trying to think. What *was* right? Or was there only a choice of wrongs? Perhaps Lark . . .

James suddenly dropped his hands and lifted his head with a new and more urgent sense of shock. *What* had Lark said? Go to Scotland? James leaped to his feet. It hadn't penetrated at the moment, but there was no doubt whatever that she would try to do exactly that.

He raced out of the chamber, along the narrow corridor, and down two flights of stairs to the kitchen where Doll was working. "Where's Lark?" he demanded.

Doll looked surprised. "I don't know; isn't she upstairs?"

"Oh, 'steeth!" James moaned. "She's done it; I knew she had!" He stood perfectly still for an instant, strongly tempted to let her go to Scotland, and be done with her once and for all. As if he hadn't enough problems on his mind right now without having to go rescue Lark—again!—from the consequences of her own willfulness!

Then his inconveniently strong sense of responsibility arose within him, reminding him that she was, for all her mulishness, a very small and helpless young person. Moreover, it added pointedly, it wasn't *always* James who did the rescuing.

James tightened his lips and started for the front door.

Doll, moving with surprising speed, stood in front of

him. "What is it?" she demanded. "Where are you going?"

"Lark's started off for Scotland!" snapped James. "I've got to stop her and bring her back!" He tried to go around the massive bulk of the cook, but Doll, simply not taking in the bit of nonsense about Scotland, moved in front of him again.

"Are you going to forget your duty for a spoiled wretch of a girl?" she demanded accusingly. "Your king needs you!"

James groaned aloud, and then most unfairly took his anger out on Doll. "I haven't forgotten my duty to anyone!" he blazed furiously. "I'll decide what my duty is, and I'll remember it, and I'll do it the best I can, and I don't need you or any other bird-witted female to tell me what it is! Now, get out of my way!"

He moved toward the door again with a look on his face that caused Doll to move hastily aside. But, far from seeming upset at his rudeness, she stared after him with what almost looked like a satisfied smile.

11

The Son of Dr. Thornybramble

Lark turned left at the corner and started down the hill leading away from the town gate—glancing over her shoulder as she did so to see if James was following her yet. Not that she expected him to do so, she told herself, slowing down a little and shifting her bag on her shoulder. She was, she added to herself, thoughtfully removing herself from his presence so that he could go off and fight his odious old war, and not have to trouble himself about her.

"Do you know what leeches are?" The question echoed so loudly in her mind that she stopped and looked around for an instant, half expecting to see Doll. Then she started down the hill, more slowly. Was she being a leech? Was she being childish and unreasonable, as James had said? Lark tried very hard to tell herself that she wasn't any of these disagreeable things, but some innate core of self-honesty raised its head and began nagging at her in a most uncomfortable way.

She swallowed and slowed down a little. She didn't much care any more for the notion of going to Scotland alone, anyway—it no longer seemed very practical or even very enjoyable. She slowed down a little more. Perhaps this was, after all, the wrong way to keep James from going off and getting himself killed in battle? Perhaps, instead, she should talk to him, reasonably and convincingly. Perhaps she should even go back now, and say she was sorry? She hated having quarreled with him! It made her feel quite sick, as if she'd eaten something that disagreed with her.

She stopped in the road, staring at the cobblestones, more than half minded to turn back at once. And then she heard a horridly familiar voice squawk "Elizabeth!" and heavy hands grabbed her arms.

Lark didn't need to look up. The hands that held her and the voice in her ears were unmistakably and revoltingly those of Will-of-God!

"Elizabeth!" he bleated. "What in the name of heaven are you doing *here?* How did you come? Where's Mother? How did you *get* here, Elizabeth?"

Lark looked up at last, and the expression on her face was the most idiotic she had ever worn. This time it was not an act. She was simply paralyzed. For once her quick-thinking mind was a total blank, and she could not think of any faintly probable reason for anything at all.

"Elizabeth!" Will shook her. "What is the matter with you? You look fair half-witted! How did you get here, I say?"

Lark's mind clicked back into working order at this cue, and she immediately looked as half-witted as possible.

"Who are you?" she squeaked. "Let go of me! I don't know you, and my name isn't Elizabeth!"

Will-of-God looked confused but stubborn. Lark realized that she probably couldn't convince him that she wasn't herself. But if he believed she had lost her wits . . . "My name's Lark, and you're a horrid boy, and I don't like you at all," she said with great feeling. "Let go of me."

Will-of-God did no such thing. He took a firmer grip, if anything. "Don't you know me, Elizabeth?" he demanded indignantly, putting his face down near hers so that she could get a better look at it.

She shuddered and indicated that the sight made her sick. And even beneath her fright, some part of her mind was very much enjoying the chance to let Will-of-God know what she thought of him.

"Ugh!" she said.

"Elizabeth! I'm your cousin Will-of-God, remember? I'm going to marry you when you grow up, Elizabeth," he added, but with a note of uncertainty. He was beginning to think that perhaps it had been a mistake about God willing their marriage—or, more likely, He had changed His mind and was now indicating His disapproval by afflicting her with madness. Or perhaps she was possessed by Satan? Will looked distinctly alarmed.

Lark perceived this doubt and immediately set about encouraging it. Feeble-mindedness seemed a small price to pay for getting out of marrying Will. "I wouldn't marry you for anything!" she declared, trying to get away, and making horrible faces at him. "You're a wicked, horrid, disgusting young man, and the Devil is in you, and I never saw you before in my life."

"Elizabeth!" repeated Will-of-God, deeply shocked.

He stared at her silently for a moment, trying to decide what on earth to do about her. "I shall have to take you to Captain Dove," he decided finally. "He'll put you somewhere safe until Father gets back from Bristol." And he began walking her back up the hill.

Will was strong, and there was no use at all fighting him. Lark struggled just as a matter of principle, with no hope of getting loose. And then her heart jumped. A figure appeared from the side street at the top of the hill, and it was James. He was staring at them, and Lark was seized with terror for him. He must not get himself in trouble! How could she warn him?

James was starting down the hill toward them with a most ominously calm look on his face. Lark twisted around to face Will, and raised her voice. "I don't care if you *do* say you're my cousin!" she shouted. "*I* say you're a toad and a dog, and I never saw you before, so a hey nonny nonny to you, too!"

She turned from the baffled Will toward James, who was now hesitating, clearly trying to figure out the situation before setting about the murder he had in mind. Two other Roundhead soldiers, across the street, turned to watch the scene with great interest, and James realized that he must be astute. He looked at Lark for more clues.

She obligingly pointed at him. "And you," she declared, "are a clever brown fox, and I never saw you in my life, either. He—" She jerked her head at Will. "—says I'm his cousin Elizabeth, but I'm not; I'm a lark, and all those other soldiers are boars and weasels, and they bite."

She looked at James, hoping that he would get the idea. And James, although still confused, understood very well that Lark was warning him. He looked at the hulking and bucktoothed young man holding her. Cousin, had she said? Things began to clarify a little.

"She *is* my cousin," said Will-of-God, looking at James's sober garments and assuming that he was a Puritan and therefore a friend. "I can't think how she got here from back home near Salisbury, but God has clearly smitten her with madness. I suppose it's because she came from a vile Royalist home, and has never been saved."

"Saved, saved, saved," sang Lark, trying to sound as mad as possible, just to make sure James got the point.

James got it, and was thinking as hard as he could. This should have been the answer to at least one of his big problems. Let Lark's own relatives take care of her, which they could quite likely do better than James. They would certainly keep her safe, at the very least, and James was not at all certain he could do that much. To be sure, she would probably be well punished for her naughtiness—but at the moment James was inclined to think that a little punishment was richly deserved, and would probably be of great benefit to her character. Moreover, considering that James did have other pressing obligations, this would certainly be the practical solution all around.

James's mind told him all this, but his feelings persisted in being quite irrational and unscientific. He had not the least intention of abandoning Lark to her detestable relations, and although he called himself all kinds of fool, it did not at all change his mind.

On the other hand, how was he to manage a rescue? The two Puritan soldiers were crossing the road now to see what was happening. And it was quite clear that James could not help Lark by getting himself killed or beaten up or imprisoned. So he looked at Will mildly.

"What will you do with her?"

Will looked discouraged. "I'll have to ask my captain to lock her up until my father gets back, I suppose. Father is Colonel Jeremiah Talbot," he added, bragging a little. "He'll take care of everything, and he should be back in a few days now."

James considered this. Then he shook his head and made a clucking sound at Will.

"Very awkward," he pointed out. "In a few days the Black Boy and his savage Scots will be here, no doubt, and what can you do with a little girl in the middle of a battle?" Will looked more depressed than ever, and James pursued his advantage before the young man could remember his father again. "And in the meantime," he said, "where will you keep her? Surely not in a garrison of soldiers! That would not be at all fitting for a little maid, even a young and feeble-witted one."

"Loud sing cuckoo," remarked Lark, thankful that James was apparently not going to get himself killed on the spot, and quite sure that he would rescue her by sheer brilliance and scientific logic. She smiled cheerfully. The other two soldiers were now standing behind Will and staring, and Will's shoulders were drooping.

"I'll take her to Captain Dove," he repeated doggedly.

Lark looked at him with loathing. "I don't know if I ought to associate with you," she said. "Your eyes are too close together, and you have pimples, and I feel quite sure that Satan is in you."

Will-of-God had never tolerated any kind of back talk

from anyone smaller than himself. His arm automatically lifted. James's own arm shot out even faster, and he took a firm hold of Will's wrist. He smiled and shook his head gently, very thankful that he had acted in time, because if Will had struck Lark, James would have reduced him to very small pieces in short order, and regardless of consequences. It was true that Lark needed her ears boxed, but James strongly felt that *he* was the one to attend to it. And in any case, it wouldn't be for impudence to her cousin.

"Tut-tut!" he murmured reprovingly, while Will stared with open mouth, and the other two soldiers peered with furrowed brows over his shoulders. "You must never strike or scold anyone with wandering wits," chided James solemnly. "It could have quite awful effects."

Will began to frown heavily, and James called upon his imagination. "You see," he explained with an air of great knowledge, "I just happen to know rather a lot about these cases. *My* father," he added impressively, "is *the* Dr. Theophilus Thornybramble."

Lark giggled. Fortunately this was put down to her madness and no one paid any attention. Will and the two heads over his shoulders were looking both blank and awed. They had never heard of Dr. Theophilus Thornybramble, of course, since James had just finished inventing him, but it was clear to them that they *ought* to have heard of him, and that only the most shocking ignoramus could fail to recognize the name instantly. No one wanted to admit to such ignorance, so they all nodded and looked impressed.

"You've heard, of course, of the important work he has done in this field," James went on, beginning rather to enjoy himself in spite of the danger. At least he now had his feet on the ground, with no doubt at all of where his duty lay. Moreover, here was a battle he could fight with his favorite weapon—his wits.

He flickered his eyes ever so slightly at Lark, who winked back at him and then crossed her eyes at Will-of-God and began to gnaw at the middle of one braid as if it were a bone.

"You see," said James, "such attacks of madness can be caused by a melancholia or sometimes a demon, which seizes upon the outer layer of brain. The soul immediately sets up a barrier to keep it from going any further, and if the victim is treated with great kindness, this barrier can strengthen and move outwards, thus displacing the demon or melancholia in time. But any kind of ill treatment can cause the barrier to collapse like the outer wall of a castle, leaving the citadel at the mercy of the attacker. And on occasion," he finished ominously, "the soul has no time to escape, and is trapped."

"Bang, bang," remarked Lark, nodding briskly.

The head over Will's left shoulder blinked and retreated an inch. The eyes over his right shoulder rounded even more. But Will-of-God, although most impressed with such learned discourse, was not distracted from his purpose. "I won't hit her if she's polite," he conceded grudgingly. "Now let's take her to Captain Dove."

James, who still had no very clear idea of his plan of attack, agreed for lack of a better idea. The small procession marched up the hill and down the other side, with Will and James on either side of Lark and the two soldiers trailing along behind.

Captain Dove had been at the top of the castle, helping plan for battle—just in case the coming one should take place here. It worried him, particularly since he was responsible to Colonel Talbot, and he was not in the least pleased at being called down by the colonel's dull-skulled son and presented with the sort of problem that he just was not prepared to face. None of his training had given him the least notion of what to do with a girl child who had lost her wits, particularly if she happened to be the future daughter-in-law of his own superior officer.

He glowered heavily at the group before him, and looked around the gloomy stone walls for inspiration. There was none there. He looked at Lark, who stuck out her tongue at him. It gave her great satisfaction to be as impudent as she liked to the Roundheads, and get away with it. She put her tongue back in and made a horrible face. Captain Dove looked away again hastily.

"Well, what do you expect me to do with her?" he inquired irritably.

Will-of-God indicated that he didn't know, and implied that it was now the captain's responsibility. The captain almost swore, remembered himself just in time, and seethed quietly for a moment.

"Do you want leave to take her back home or to Bedlam or somewhere?" he asked with heavy restraint.

"Oh, no!" objected Will, who had been very much looking forward to his first battle. "Can't we just lock her up until Father comes back?"

"Now where," asked Captain Dove, "do you think *I* could keep her? In one of the dungeons?"

"I suppose so," agreed Will vaguely.

The captain, looking shocked, demanded whether Will had ever seen one of the dungeons, and whether he really wanted his future bride put there. Will-of-God looked highly uncomfortable, but more at the thought of his marriage than the dungeons. James cleared his throat modestly.

"If you'll forgive me, sir?" he suggested, and they all looked at him.

"Who are you?" Captain Dove asked guardedly.

"Oh, he's the son of the famous—uh—Dr. Thruthlethwaite," put in one of the Roundhead soldiers.

Captain Dove stared from under shaggy eyebrows. "Who?"

"Horatio Thornybramble, son of Dr. Theophilus Thornybramble, at your service, sir," said James, bowing. "I see that you are a man of intellect, and I should be happy to put my own limited knowledge at your disposal."

The captain regarded him doubtfully. "Who?" he repeated, being a man who was not in the least embarrassed about his own abysmal ignorance. "Never heard of the fellow."

James was by now prepared for this. One could not expect a bluff to work indefinitely. "Your profession is in quite a different field, of course," he murmured politely. "However, if you should ever care to consult the Calvin Academy of Mental Infirmaties in Geneva, or the Martin Luther College for Study of Divine and Malignant Affliction in Stockholm, I think you would find my father's name well known and greatly admired."

Captain Dove knew nothing (fortunately) about such intellectual subjects, but he did know the names Luther and Calvin, which was precisely what James had counted on. He looked considerably friendlier, and permitted James to repeat his little speech about madness, with improvements.

"Ha—hmm," he remarked at last, remembering that his time was valuable. He really had no interest at all in Will-of-God or his unfortunate future bride, but he had considerable interest in avoiding the wrath of Colonel Talbot. "Well, Master Thornycroft, and what would you suggest?" he asked.

"Thornybramble," corrected James gravely. "I should suggest, sir, that as you so astutely point out, a garrison—particularly if it may soon be involved in a battle—is no place for the child. However, I happen to be staying at the Word-of-God Inn at the top of the town. The proprietress is a fine, godly woman, as you no doubt know, and I dare say she would be willing to take charge of the poor little creature temporarily. In addition, I would even be willing to try to effect a cure—although it may be that my skill is not equal to it, and she should be taken to my father."

Captain Dove looked relieved. Will-of-God did not. "Who would pay for the room?" he asked. "I don't think anyone ought to meddle with Elizabeth until Father gets back, except me, of course. I'm her cousin, you know."

"You are not my cousin!" shouted Lark, deciding it was time for her to make another contribution. "I don't like that man!" she told the captain confidingly. "If I have to see him again, I shall scream and scream."

"Elizabeth!" bleated Will-of-God, very much mortified.

"Oh, for—" Captain Dove swallowed some words

which General Cromwell would most certainly not have approved. He restrained himself from telling Lark that she showed remarkably good sense, mad or not, and that he might scream and scream himself, if he had to see much more of Colonel Talbot's pimply son. He breathed deeply. "I can't stand here all day with this," he said finally, through his teeth. "Take her up to the inn, for the love of heaven. I'll stand the bill if necessary. And you get right back here, Private Talbot. You're not on leave, you know."

Half an hour later Lark was securely locked in a small room near the top of the inn, with a short chain on the casement window. James was down in the kitchen fuming, and Will-of-God was back at the castle, presumably. James wished him in a much warmer place. All had gone so well, he growled, pacing the kitchen, until that wretched knot-head had insisted on keeping the key to Lark's room himself!

James groaned.

12
The Prisoner

"It's idiotic not to have another key!" said James. "Any inn has got to have extra keys!"

Doll shrugged and went on kneading dough in what James considered a heartless manner. He sat down at the white-scrubbed table and regarded her with disfavor. Why on earth had she permitted Lark to be locked in that room if it only had one key? It was hard to believe that she could be so careless. Surely she couldn't be a Roundhead spy? No, that was quite impossible. But why was she so unconcerned about Lark?

"Well, what are we going to do?" he demanded hotly. "How are we going to get her out? What if the inn should burn down?" (He had also asked this of Will-of-God, who had merely looked blank and pointed out that it never had burned down, so why should it now?) "*Do* something, Doll!"

Doll punched the dough vigorously and looked calm. "Don't be such a hothead, James Trelawney. Your little friend is safe enough for the time being, and how safe do you think anyone would be if her Roundhead relations find her gone? For that matter, where do you think you could take her?"

"I—" began James, and paused, because he hadn't got quite that far yet in his plans.

"Why not leave well enough alone for a few days?" Doll went on. "Don't forget, King Charles and his army may be passing by here any day now, and you'll need to be free to join him; and then there's bound to be a battle soon, and everything may settle itself."

James's mind had to admit that there was some sense in this, but again his feelings were stronger. Besides, he was getting a very irritating feeling that everyone was trying to run his life and make his decisions for him. As a result, he didn't feel like taking anyone's advice, however sensible.

Not being able to say all this to Doll, he scowled. "It's a terrible idea," he told her perversely. "Besides, you can't keep a little girl locked up like that; it isn't decent."

Doll looked at him oddly and hardened her face. "Well, she *is* locked in," she pointed out unanswerably. "Besides, even if we could let her out, she'd probably just run away again, and—" Doll wisely broke off her sentence just there and let James complete it in his mind for himself.

James was silent, having no difficulty at all in completing the thought. It was quite true that Lark was not exactly the hapless angel-in-distress of romantic tales, but a lively and independent girl, to say the least of it. Still, he couldn't just abandon her, although Doll seemed almost to think he should.

He looked at her stolid face, single-purposed and stern. Doll never was tormented by divided loyalties, choices of wrongs. She gave her loyalty simply and unquestioningly, would sacrifice herself or anyone else for the king's cause. James had never met a person of such iron purpose, and it shook him. He covered his eyes with his hand. The question of this morning swept over him. What was right? Was he weak and disloyal, that he couldn't accept things without question?

Doll pressed her advantage. "You're a young idealist, and not very practical," she said kindly. "You can't see the forest for the trees. What does one tree more or less matter? It's the good of the forest that counts."

James considered this warily. It sounded sensible, but he didn't trust it. "No!" he said suddenly. "There's a great big hole in your logic, Doll!"

Doll, being a tidy housekeeper, looked distressed at the very idea of a hole.

"The forest *is* trees," said James firmly. "They all matter. Human beings matter even more. Surely that's what life is all about? Didn't Jesus keep saying over and over that we must care about people? All people!"

Doll began slapping her dough into pans for rising. "Jesus didn't have Cromwell to worry about," she pointed out. "Where would we be if we went around turning the other cheek? Sometimes we have to sacrifice a few people for the good of all. It's the goal that counts, no matter how you get there."

James shook his head, and pushed his chair back suddenly, so that it grated harshly against the stone flags. He went over and stared into the fire for a few minutes. Then he shook his head again.

"No good," he said. "You're saying we sometimes have to do evil to achieve good, but it doesn't work. That's Cromwell's excuse for butchering helpless women and children in Ireland. That's the excuse men have always made for doing the most ghastly cruel things. You can't use black paint and expect to paint a wall white with it!" James turned around and looked at Doll pleadingly. "We can't ever be *sure* that our actions will have good results, we can only do things that we *hope* will come out right—so it's really what we *do* that's important. And you can't do evil to get good, because it will turn out evil; can't you see that, Doll? . . . And none of this," he added vehemently, "is helping Lark!"

Doll shook her head. She couldn't see his point at all. "Nor the King," she said. "Talk talk talk—but what he needs is men to fight for him, not fuss about whether it's right."

They looked at each other, stalemated.

Upstairs in her small prison, Lark was beginning to feel less cheerful again. She had assumed that James would come let her out the minute Will-of-God left, and they would set off immediately for some safer place, like Devon. But it must surely be nearly an hour now since Will had stumped off, and where was James? What could have happened?

Lark had managed to think of at least twenty terrible

possibilities before she finally heard his footsteps up the creaky steep stairs. She flew to the door, expecting to hear a key turn in the lock, but instead there was a cautious tap, and then James's voice in the large empty keyhole.

"Lark? Are you all right?"

"Of course!" Lark cried. "Are *you* all right? What happened? Let me out!"

"Shhh. I can't. Speak softly, Lark; there are Roundheads staying here, remember. Lark, Will took the only key away with him."

There was a short silence while Lark digested this. "Can't you get me out any other way?" she asked, her voice rising a little with alarm. "What about the window? James—"

"Shhh!" said James again. "Listen, Lark, it isn't going to be as easy as that. For one thing, where do we go when we get you out? We can't just walk out the town gate past the castle and garrison, and I don't know a good hiding place in Shrewsbury yet."

Lark's heart sank, but not too far, for James was there. "Aren't there any other Royalists in town?" she asked practically.

"Oh, yes," James agreed, thanking heaven that Lark was being sensible. "I'll find something eventually. But in the meantime, the safest thing is to leave you here."

"But what about Uncle Jeremiah?" Lark's voice broke into a squeak of alarm.

"I know." James sounded altogether too calm for Lark's liking. "I've been thinking about that, too. But I don't think he can do anything much when he does come; not right away, anyhow. After all, he won't have much time, with armies heading this way. I doubt if he'll even take you away from here, Lark. Where else could he put you?"

"With some Roundhead friend in town," suggested Lark promptly and unhappily.

James shifted his position slightly, for the keyhole was at an awkward height. "That's what they think Doll is," he reminded her. "It should seem quite logical just to leave you here."

There was a stricken silence from inside the room, while Lark contemplated the wreckage of what only yesterday had seemed a fairly rosy future. Now she was locked in a small room whose walls kept threatening to close in on her. Uncle Jeremiah loomed ominously in the near future—and, worst of all, James was beginning to sound like Doll! No doubt he was still perfectly determined to run off and meet a gory death in battle too. Lark shivered. Even the thought of having to face Uncle Jeremiah—though it made her very bones go wobbly with dismay—paled beside James's danger. And it seemed she was helpless to prevent it.

Then Lark pulled herself together. She must somehow contrive to save them both, since James seemed to have no intention of doing so. In a way, this was all her own fault, for being so stupid earlier today. If she hadn't run off in a huff, she might never have run into Will-of-God at all. And of course flying into a temper with James had been the worst way in the world to persuade him of anything, however much it was for his own good. Grandmother had told her that many a time. Now it was going to be excessively difficult to win him over to her viewpoint. It never occurred to Lark that perhaps it was none of her business, much less that she might be wrong. She wished only good for her James, and she was perfectly certain that she knew best how he should attain it.

With this in mind, Lark took herself in hand. Courage and a cool head were needed. And tact, for James must not know he was being managed, men being quite peculiar about things like that. She sternly subdued the panic that gripped her at the very thought of her uncle, and controlled a strong desire to bleat at James through the keyhole. She marshaled her wits.

"Lark?" James's voice sounded a trifle worried at the prolonged silence.

Lark swallowed hard. "Yes, James," she managed in a voice intended to be calm and brave, but which sounded small and forlorn. "Whatever you say, James."

The desolation in her voice nearly undid James, but the unnatural meekness of her words caused him to slant a suspicious eyebrow in the direction of the keyhole and grin wryly. So that was it, was it? The frontal attack hadn't worked, so now it would be a flank movement. What a transparent child she was, really—once a person was on to her.

"Doing it rather too brown, aren't you?" he murmured at the door.

"What did you say, James?"

James didn't enlighten her. Neither did he comfort her very much. For one thing, having once decided she was putting on an act, James didn't in the least realize how truly strongly she felt about having to confront Uncle Jeremiah. And for another, he was inclined to want to punish her just a little bit for her behavior earlier and her probable intentions for the future.

"Have you got plenty to eat in there?" he asked. "We

can let something down from the roof, I dare say, if you should run out before your odious cousin comes back with his cursed key." James had developed an immediate and intense dislike for Will-of-God.

Lark giggled shakily. "Doll put enough food and water in here for a large family," she told him. "And I'd as lief Will didn't come back at all, even with the key," she added, achieving the light-hearted touch with some effort.

"Oh, he will," James predicted darkly. "And," he added, with just the slightest touch of malice, "you'd better save some of your acting ability to use on him. I don't mean insulting him, either. I know that's satisfying, but you'll just make him angrier, and it's better if he's puzzled and a little sorry for you. Be as pathetic and idiotic as you can. You know what I mean. Cry. Be afraid of him."

"All right," Lark agreed reluctantly. And when Will-of-God returned, early that evening, she played her part as effectively as James could have wished.

Will, definitely shaken, left the room fairly quickly, locked the door, and turned a disturbed face to the impassive James. "Do you think it's the Lord or the Devil who has afflicted her?" he asked, almost humbly—for Will.

James looked wisely thoughtful. "It's a bit too soon to say," he declared, leading the way down the narrow stairs. "I do think perhaps you shouldn't keep asking her how she got here, though. She probably doesn't know, and you see how it upsets her. I do wish you would entrust the proprietress with the key, Master Talbot. I worry about fire, and in any case, it might be that we could help her somewhat."

Will-of-God was looking both annoyed and bewildered as he thought of Elizabeth's behavior. "I don't understand it," he muttered shaking his large cropped head. "Why should she fear or dislike me?"

James maintained a rather grim silence at this, hoping that Will might remember a few reasons why. Nothing of the sort happened, of course. Will did not even know he was a bully. He thought of himself as a fine fellow, one of the Superior Sex, and of those Elected To Salvation; and he thought he had always treated Lark rather better than she deserved.

"Perhaps I pampered and spoiled her too much at home?" he suggested. "Father always said she needed more discipline."

James controlled his impulses. "Not now, I fear," he said judiciously, turning at the front door to look gravely into the stolid face of Will. "Uh—about the key—"

Will-of-God looked at him. "I'll ask Father when he comes back," he said stiffly, and left.

James's next remarks were not intended for his ears, and it was just as well they didn't reach them.

The next five days furnished both Lark and James plenty of time for a great deal of thinking. It was not altogether pleasant for either of them. Lark hated being closed in, to begin with. A Greek student might have called it claustrophobia; Lark knew only that she kept wanting to knock down the walls which pressed in on her, and sometimes she sat and fought with herself for what seemed hours, to keep from screaming. And even when she wasn't busy not screaming, her thoughts were not very cheerful.

At first she felt very hurt and cross about James, who was suddenly no longer a combination of fond playmate and chivalrous knight, but rather more like a brisk but unadoring older brother. Lark blamed Doll for this. She had influenced him, and that was something only Lark was supposed to do.

But Lark's mind had a tendency to look for logic whether Lark's feelings liked it or not. Now it began to follow a relentless train of thought which she found exceedingly unpleasant, because it came to the distressing conclusion that she, Elizabeth Lark Lennox, had been guilty of a number of things. She had been babyish and selfish and unreasonable. Worse, she had been so delighted to get her own way about things that she had expected James always to do exactly as she wanted—and he a grown-up man, practically, and about the king's business!

Even all alone in her prison, Lark hid her face in her hands as the awfulness of her behavior slowly sank in. No wonder James had turned a bit testy! It was really, she decided humbly, astonishingly noble of him to have rescued her from Will-of-God at all, and she must show her gratitude by reforming at once. As soon as he saved her from Uncle Jeremiah, she would be simply unbelievably sweet and meek, and never try to dictate to him in the least, but go to Devon or wherever he wished, except, of course, to battle.

Lark realized with some chagrin that she wasn't really reforming at all, but only deciding to be nice as long as she had her own way. If she wanted James's good opinion and affection, she must not make any conditions, but truly leave all the decisions up to him, even if he should decide to leave her here and go join the King's army.

But Lark balked at that. It was too much. Besides, what good was James's good opinion if she was back with Aunt Judith and he dead on a battlefield? If she were really brave and patriotic and unselfish, of course, she would wave and smile as he went, as Mother had waved and smiled when Lark's father and brother went. Lark decided sadly that she was not brave and patriotic and unselfish. She would try to learn to be these things, but she would have to start on something smaller, like not trying to twist James around her finger any more—or at least, not on unimportant matters.

She sighed. Growing up was turning out to be quite as complicated and difficult as she had suspected it would be.

James still wrestled with his awful dilemma about loyalty, and tried to figure out how to rescue Lark. Sometimes he argued with himself, and sometimes with Doll, and occasionally with Will-of-God. None of it seemed to help much.

In the meantime, Shrewsbury waited for the Scottish army to arrive, and Cromwell behind it, while the garrison at the castle wondered what had delayed Colonel Talbot's return. Will-of-God became more and more sullen, for the story was all over town about the half-witted child whom he claimed as his betrothed, and he found this extremely embarrassing. He began to dislike his cousin very much, and to wish Satan would fly away with her and be done with it.

When he had finally stayed away from the inn for two days altogether, Doll put on a shawl and marched down to the castle for a word with Captain Dove. Did Talbot intend to starve his little cousin, she demanded? She didn't mind keeping the child safely locked up, it being all, in a manner of speaking, for the Cause of Cromwell and God, but she drew the line at child-slaughter, and it was two days now since she had been able to get food and water in.

Doll neglected to mention, of course, that what with the wide crack under the door and a pole across from the window in the next chamber, Lark was in no danger of starving. Captain Dove, not knowing this, was as horrified as she had planned him to be. He roared for Will-of-God and ordered him to give the key to Doll at once. And Will-of-God, muttering about What His Father Would Say, obeyed.

Doll bore the key triumphantly back—not to the waiting hands of James, but into some mysterious depths of the inn. When she appeared again the key was not to be seen, and she was wearing an air of virtue victorious.

That night she and James had a long, low-voiced, and heated discussion in the privacy of the fireplace alcove. At the end of it, Doll looked more triumphant than ever, and James very meek and defeated. He almost overdid it. It was a mercy Doll didn't know him any better than she did. Lark would have perceived instantly that he was Up To Something.

But Doll went to bed happy in the thought that she had led the nice lad back to a sense of his proper duty, and at the same time made sure of one more soldier for King Charles. It was a pity she had to use a sort of blackmail to do it, but if people didn't see the Right for themselves, then it was necessary to force it upon them. And he had given in without too much struggle once she had threatened to keep

Lark locked up until he did. She went to sleep with a sense of having done a good deed that day.

James was awake for quite a long time planning, and thinking how ironic it was that he was now having to struggle against his own side as well as the enemy. Of course, he admitted fairly to himself, Doll might be perfectly right. James frankly didn't know. But he did know that he was *not* going to be forced into anything, right or not. He had to make up his own mind, and that he certainly couldn't do with Lark a hostage.

Doll meant well, of course, he knew. She had worked everything out in a simply splendid plan, except for just a few minor details such as trying to run James's life for him. James was sick and tired of having assorted females of various ages trying to run his life for him. He was a good-natured sort of person who liked to be obliging and to make people happy, but there was, he felt, a limit. Doll was about to discover this. And once he got Lark safely away from that brute of a cousin and an uncle who was probably just like him, Lark, too, was due for a few surprises.

James returned to his plans for the immediate future, and it was at least two more hours before he fell asleep.

13
Under the Wall

The next day dawned as if it had just remembered that this was still August, after several days doubt. A glorious radiance of sun poured into Lark's casement windows, accompanied by the golden-green smells of a hot morning. Lark put her small face close to the narrow opening permitted by the chain, and reflected that the walls did not seem nearly as close and threatening in the sunshine.

A few minutes later the key turned in the lock, and to her surprise Doll came in alone, bearing a large tray of food balanced against one hip, and a bundle under her arm.

Lark hardly noticed these. "Isn't Will here?" she breathed cautiously, one eye on the door which had closed behind Doll. "Then you have a key now? Can I get out? What happened?"

"Tsss," Doll remarked, setting the tray down on the table. "Be patient, girl. I have the key, but you can't leave now; surely you can see that." She looked at Lark with severity, and then went on quite kindly. "But I'll see you have three good hot meals a day now, and plenty of water, and I've brought things to help pass the time. Here's some knitting, and both of my own books, and my old rag doll, and scraps and needle and thread so that you can make clothing for her. And I'll bring up cleaning things later. As long as you're here, you may as well keep the room tidy."

She hurried off, leaving Lark both encouraged and a little confused. Doll had never been this kind before. But she didn't seem to know whether Lark was a child who played with dolls or a young lady who read Shakespeare. Lark preferred the latter. It was a novelty after two years with Uncle Jeremiah, and besides, reading helped take her mind from thinking and walls that closed in.

It was nearly noon when she heard James hiss at the keyhole and flew over to talk to him. "Are you all right?" he breathed softly. "Lark, listen: we're going to try to get away tonight."

"Tonight?" Lark whispered. "But Doll said—"

"I know she did," said James grimly. "We're running away from her as well as the Roundheads now. I'll explain later. She's at market now; we'll have to plan quickly. It's going to be hard, because she keeps the key hidden. I can't think of anything except just to try to make her give it to me—even if I have to—" He stopped, very much afraid it would not work. He couldn't think of any way to make her tell, even if he were willing to kill her, which of course he wasn't. "Do you have any other ideas at all?" he asked Lark, but without much hope.

"Couldn't I go out the window?" asked Lark calmly.

For a moment James thought perhaps her wits *had* turned. "With that chain on it?" he demanded. "I looked at that when they put you in there. You can't possibly open the casement more than six inches."

"I don't know how many inches it is," returned Lark, "but it's exactly as wide as my head, and my head is quite small. If I scrape my ears a little and then turn sideways for the rest of me, I can get through quite easily. I've already gone half through twice—but just at night," she added hastily, thinking James's silence might mean that she had been imprudent.

Actually, he was busy seeing their escape in a whole new perspective, and also feeling a great admiration for Lark's ingenuity and courage. He did not at all care for heights, himself. It didn't occur to him that Lark was perfectly comfortable in high places, and it hadn't required any courage at all for her to stick herself half out. On the contrary, she would have dared much more to escape those awful in-pressing walls.

"I think it might work," he whispered after a minute. "The room under you is empty; Doll saw to that. It isn't so far down, but how could you do it? You can't climb a rope, can you?"

Lark considered this. "I expect I could climb down a sheet," she suggested. "In the stories Gran used to tell me, people usually climbed down sheets or ivy. Besides, I can cut little holes in the sheet for my fingers and toes. It's good stout linen."

James had a sudden vision of Lark clinging to a frail sheet on the sheer wall of the inn. How could he have considered such a thing? Better to have her stay a prisoner and safe, even if it should mean going back to her uncle. He would not consider risking her life! Very much upset, he explained this to the keyhole.

The keyhole immediately began to sputter and hiss in such a fury that James drew back a little and eyed it with disapproval. Really, she could be an *extremely* difficult person to handle!

On the other side of the door, Lark caught an echo of his thoughts, and her sputtering stopped abruptly as she clapped both hands over her mouth. Here she was behaving like a very shrew—and after all her good resolutions, too! How wicked and stupid of her!

She peered anxiously through the large keyhole and caught a glimpse of an angry brown eye peering back at her. "I'm sorry, James," she said so humbly that James was thrown off his stride with surprise. "I'll do whatever you say."

James recovered at once, and decided—most unfairly this time—that she was just using guile again. It wasn't going to work, he decided with some amusement, and set about devising another plan at once.

Disconcertingly, Lark agreed to everything he proposed, so that he descended the steep stairs a few minutes later in some confusion. Perhaps he had misjudged her? At any rate, she was certainly a surprising small person, and perhaps he was lucky to have such a practical and gallant companion in adventure. All their plans were made for getting out, and now he needed to explore the town a bit and see if he could figure out the best way of getting outside the wall.

Downstairs he met Doll just returning from market. "Any news?" he asked casually. "I've been waiting for you to get back. I want to wander around and pick up rumor myself. No word of the king?"

Doll shook her head. "I've decided to move into the room just beneath Lark," she said, equally casual. "Then if she should need anything during the night, she can just knock on her floor. I should have thought of it sooner."

Her eyes were very bright as they looked at James, and he knew quite well that she had a different reason for her move. He stood still and hoped he hadn't gone pale. "Yes, I should think you ought," he agreed with a show of indignation. "I said so from the first. What if the inn caught fire or something? I'll go up and tell her now; she'll feel less lonely just knowing."

Doll nodded, and James fled upstairs to whisper the shattering news into the keyhole. "I'll try to think of something else," he promised. "If I get a plan I may have to slip a note under the door. You be thinking, too."

And then he went out into the sunny town quickly, because he really didn't want to talk to Doll just now, and also because he had a good deal of thinking to do. He wandered around the streets closest to the town wall, one eye open for a place where it might be possible to climb over. The other eye was turned inward on a mental picture of the attic just over Lark's room, and the arrangement of the casements. He had the beginning of a plan, but it seemed even more dangerous than the first one.

The town wall was beginning to look extremely discouraging. There seemed to be no trees conveniently close, and as a matter of fact, it was difficult to get very near the wall at all, since there were walled back gardens right up against it almost all the way around town. It was not at all promising, and James began to cast around in his mind for some other way out of Shrewsbury.

But then in a narrow street in a shabby section, he saw a bit of garden wall next to the town wall that was crumbled in one spot. James sauntered on very casually, but his sharp eye noticed that the house belonging to that garden had a vaguely deserted look about it, and the weeds in the cracks of that bit of wall were thriving. He yawned a little, arranged himself in a patch of shade within sight of that bit of wall, and made himself a part of the scenery until at last there was no one in sight. Then he squeezed himself through the gap, thankful that his strength was of the lean and wiry variety. If he had run to heavy bulging muscle, he would never have got through.

Inside, he found himself in a labyrinth of fallen stones and overgrown shrubs, and one or two trees—but none, he saw with a sinking heart, at all close to the town wall.

"S'teeth!" he muttered, and stood still, telling himself that he really shouldn't have hoped for such luck, anyway.

And then there was a furtive sound at the broken wall behind him, and he whirled, one hand ready to pluck out his dagger if it should be necessary.

A small girl stood surveying him with interest. Tangled hair hung over her grubby little face so that her eyes peered out from behind a black mat, and her rags were colorful but dirty. One finger went to her mouth when James turned, but she didn't budge from where she stood planted at the hole in the wall.

James stared back. It seemed to him presently that there was something faintly aggressive about the way she stood, putting him in mind of a puppy standing guard over a bone.

He cocked his head on one side and smiled down at her. "Hullo," he said. "What's your name?"

James's smile was altogether irresistible. It was white and wide, causing deep dents along his lean cheeks, and his eyes crinkled with it. This little girl—like Lark before her—was smitten with instant devotion. She wriggled ecstatically, shuffled her feet, and smiled back. "Glenna," she told him, and then remembered herself and scowled behind her hair.

"Well, Glenna," James said confidingly, "you're a very nice person, I can tell. I'm James."

Glenna, clearly making an effort not to melt, nodded with dignity, and then looked around pointedly. "What will you be doing in here, look?" she asked him hoarsely.

James looked down at the small dirty face, wondering at the challenge and hostility there. Then light dawned. "Is this your special place to play?" he asked her, and she nodded, unyielding.

"I see." He squatted down on his heels and smiled again. "Well, you need not worry about me, Glenna. I shan't disturb it. Do you mind if I just look around a little?"

Glenna was clearly in two minds about this. "There's yourself is a foreigner," she pointed out doubtfully.

"But I'm a very nice foreigner," James told her, and smiled again to prove it. "And I promise, word of honor, that I won't say one word about this place to even one single townsman."

Glenna tilted her matted head and stared shrewdly from behind her fringe. "Is it yourself is wanting it a secret, too?" she demanded.

Slightly taken aback, James blinked and then nodded.

The child went on surveying him for an instant. Then she gave a gap-toothed but engaging grin and held out a dirty hand. "It's us's secret place, look you," she said. "But you can see too."

Together they wandered around at random, James staring rather hopelessly at the not very helpful trees and the smooth high wall. Then he became aware that Glenna was carefully avoiding a certain rhododendron bush next to the wall. He tested this by turning his steps that way, and Glenna at once pulled him in another. James stopped and looked at her quizzically.

"What's the matter, Glenna?" he asked kindly.

Glenna avoided his eyes and shuffled one bare ankle against the other. Then she peered up at him again, clearly in the throes of some terribly difficult decision. Finally she heaved a great sigh, smiled, and beckoned. "Us has another secret, look you," she confided, and dived behind the sprawling rhododendron bush. James followed, his eyes gleaming. There had been a small earthslide here, it seemed, for one of the bottom blocks of the wall had slid downward and out just enough to leave a narrow tunnel. The stones above it had locked against each other, so that there was no danger of the wall collapsing.

Glenna squatted down and began scooping away some of the mud from the recent rain. Presently she flashed a gamin grin at James, lay down, and wriggled through. "Us goes out this way, look," she chirped back through the hole to James. "Come on. It's big enough, indeed."

James stooped and peered through. It seemed big enough. "Not just yet, Glenna," he called softly. "Come back now, so I can talk to you."

In a minute her mud-covered face appeared again, and she slithered out. "Why not?" she demanded.

"Not now," explained James gravely. "Perhaps another time. Is this a secret tunnel, Glenna? Who is 'us'?"

"Me and Owen," explained Glenna. "And now you. Will you go visit Wales? Indeed, and Wales is fine. Us is Welsh, look see. Will you go soon?"

"Quite soon," said James. "That is, if you keep it a secret." Glenna tossed her tangled mop to indicate that if anyone could keep a secret, she could. James believed her. "We can both keep secrets," he told her in a very flattering adult-to-adult way, as they headed back to the garden entrance. "Shall we shake hands on it?"

Glenna glowed, and grasped his hand in her grubby one. And such was her warmth and charm under the dirt that James bestowed a kiss upon her cheek when they parted with vows of eternal friendship.

Very much cheered, he set about making one or two important purchases, for his plan was now developed enough to make it seem a trifle less dangerous. He arrived back at the inn with some fifty feet of strong rope concealed under his cloak, and a little later Lark received a long note under her door, with most elaborate instructions written on it.

At about midnight that night, Doll was comfortably asleep, but several other people were not.

Colonel Jeremiah Talbot, just arrived back in Shrewsbury, was asking God with some severity why He had chosen to inflict a crazed niece on His servant just at this moment, and how on earth Elizabeth had got here at all.

Will-of-God, who had been unable to answer this question and had received a strong tongue-lashing in consequence, was awake too, smarting in spirit, and disliking Elizabeth more than ever for being the cause of it all. He had definitely decided that he did not wish to marry her, even if she recovered her wits.

Captain Dove was wondering when the expected armies were going to arrive, and if they were really going to come past Shrewsbury after all. It was also occurring to him that perhaps he should have asked that young Horatio Thornywhatsis more about himself and why he was not in the Parliament army.

Lark, half asleep with one ear pressed firmly against the door, heard James scratch it lightly on his way up to the attic, and at once became wide awake. She tiptoed shoelessly to the casement and waited for a rope to come slithering down from the window above. When it did, she tied her bag (containing shoes, caps, collars, stockings, and cloak stuffed on top) firmly to the end. Then she pushed and squeezed the bulge of it through the narrowness of the space between window and frame, and watched it moving slowly upward, bouncing a little against the side of the inn.

Presently the rope came back down, this time accompanied by another one, with knots in it a foot or so apart. Lark went to work very efficiently. It did not occur to her to be nervous about anything except waking Doll, and she certainly did not dream that James, above, was shaking like a leaf and beginning to want to forget the whole thing. She would surely fall and be battered to bits on the cobblestones below! How could he have considered letting her . . .

James leaned out to call to her, and found it was too

late. Lark had tied the end of one rope around her waist, had the end of the knotted one firmly in her hands, and was in the process of squeezing her small self through the ridiculously narrow gap.

James groaned, prayed, and took himself in hand. He began pulling gently but firmly upwards on the rope tied around Lark, keeping it just taut. If she should lose her grip on the other, her life would depend on this one. By the time Lark had scrambled in at the attic window, grinning and in high spirits, James had beads of perspiration along his upper lip, and had to sit down for a moment. Once he got Lark out of this particular mess, he was going to see to it personally that she should never again be exposed to any danger as long as she lived!

He would have been extremely aggravated had he known that Lark had just decided to share all danger and adventure with him for the rest of their lives.

But there was no time for contemplation. They still had to get out of the inn, not to mention the town. Now James discovered what it was like to escape in silence from a house in which nearly every board seemed to creak. (Lark, by now, had begun to feel that this was a way of life.) They inched their way, holding their breath as they passed near Doll's room.

And then, after eternities and a dozen scares, they were unbolting the door and slipping out into the street, which seemed quite bright after the dark of the inn.

"Whew!" breathed James, wishing he could have bolted the door again from inside. Since he couldn't, he wasted no time on it, but led off at an extremely brisk pace toward the section of town with the deserted garden.

Twice they had to flatten themselves in doorways as Roundhead soldiers passed. Once James thought he was lost, and had to stop and think, and then go back a way. But at last he found the entrance to the garden, and then the tunnel under the wall.

Lark eyed the size of the hole thoughtfully. "I'll go first," she suggested. "And then you come with your hands in front of you, so if you get stuck, I can pull."

James recognized the sense of this. They knelt down and pushed their cloaks through the gap, and then their bundles, and then Lark. She burrowed under with very little trouble, and James followed with great difficulty. Lark had to brace her feet against the wall and pull on his arms, while James scrabbled with his feet and wondered how it would feel to drown in mud. But finally he scraped through, leaving a bit of shirt and skin behind him.

They sat up and looked at each other in the faint light of the half moon. They were both slimy with mud from head to toe—but they were out of Shrewsbury. They hugged each other, laughing with relief. Then they remembered that the Roundhead garrison was extremely likely to have sentries around the walls on these tense nights, and that it would be a great pity to be caught again after all this.

They stood up, picked up their things, and began the business of leaving Shrewsbury as far behind as possible before dawn.

14
The Skirmish

When the sky paled, James found a hiding place: a small clearing on a wooded hill, where the ground had been dried by the sun. They wrapped their cloaks around them, using bag and pack for pillows, and lay down for some sleep.

Lark dozed off immediately, happy and secure. But James did not. Now that he had got past the immediate problem of rescuing Lark, the other problem of his duty rose again, just as unanswerable as ever.

He lay staring up at the gray sky, now streaked with lemon and apricot. There really did not seem to be *any* right action. The ground beneath him got harder and lumpier by the minute as he went around and around the old track. He was a Royalist, and so his loyalty should be to King Charles, who ought to be king of both England and Scotland. But the Scots were invading England! And they were Covenanters, more Puritan even than Cromwell, so that if Charles were not at their head, James would feel it his duty to fight against them. But Charles *was* at their head.

James groaned, turned over on his stomach, buried his face in the crook of his arm, and tried another tack. What *could* he do at this point? He couldn't abandon Lark even if he were sure he ought to be fighting with the king. And he couldn't leave her with anyone because he didn't have any other friends in the area—even if she would stay. And he couldn't get her to his parents in Devon and hope to be back again in time to help, even if he knew what to do. He couldn't even just ignore the whole thing and devote himself to Lark, because he would know in his heart that he was avoiding the issue, and this would cause him to dislike himself. Like Lark, James couldn't bear to be a coward.

He groaned again, unable to think of any other possibilities. Perhaps he ought to try to sleep. After all, he had been awake much of the previous night, too. But by now the birds were making a perfectly outrageous racket, shouting and twittering and yelping at the dawn as if they had never seen one before. James muttered uncomplimentary things into his bent arm, sighed, resigned himself to staying awake, and immediately fell asleep.

When Lark awoke, the sun was halfway up the sky and James was still sleeping. She decided not to wake him, because he was probably tired after being so heroic and clever, so she lay contentedly still. A slab of bright sunlight crept upward from her feet, and birds sang from the woods which grew down one side of the hill and in the valley below, crowding so close together at the bottom that she could not even glimpse the ground between. Lark hoped there might be a stream down there. She and James were both covered comically with dried mud, and it was beginning to feel uncomfortable.

James awoke when the slab of sunlight reached his eyes, and looked up to see Lark's face, looking rosy and contented and infinitely trustful. His dilemma—not in the least solved by having been slept on, pounced on him again, and he was seized with a kind of paralysis and guilt. He just grunted disagreeably in answer to Lark's chirp of greeting, sat up, rested his arms and chin on top of his knees, and began brooding darkly.

Lark sat up too, and looked at James anxiously. Clearly he was not himself, but she was not sure whether his pain was of the physical or the mental variety. And somehow his attitude discouraged her from asking. She thought it over for a minute. No doubt husbands had such moods now and then—even though she had never seen James in one before—and it was the duty of a wife to help, and perhaps this would be good practice. If she were very sweet and cheerful . . .

"Isn't it a lovely day, James?" she remarked brightly. "I love the smell of warm grass and trees, don't you? And I think you were so clever to get us away so perfectly! I wonder what Doll and Will-of-God are doing now?"

James didn't appear to hear her, and Lark began to wonder if she had done something to offend him. "Uh—Is it a secret what we're going to do next?" she asked meekly.

James made a muffled sound which might indicate either deep distress or anger. Lark began to progress from worry to indignation. If *she* had done anything as horrible as all that, the least he could do was tell her what it was. And if there were something terrible to worry about, why shouldn't he share it? Didn't he trust her any more? "I'm hungry!" she announced a trifle crossly.

James pulled himself out of his paralysis for a moment, dug into his pack, and produced some bread and cheese. It was not of the very best quality, as he had begun to wonder how long his money would last. Lark noticed this and guessed at the reason. Perhaps this was his trouble?

"I've still got my money," she told him, feeling into the bottom of her bag for it. "It's two shillings, fivepence, half penny. Here, take it. I ought to pay my share, you know."

James looked at her, but seemed not to have his mind entirely on the subject. "Oh," he said. "Oh. Thank you, Lark. I think you should carry it, though. We shouldn't have all our money in one place. Have you got a pocket or anything?" And without waiting for her answer, he lapsed again into gloom.

Lark, by now definitely piqued, silently fastened the little purse to her waist just under the brown skirt. She made a point of showing an immodest amount of petticoat, hoping at least to shock James into some sort of reaction; but he didn't even seem to see her. She lapsed into gloom herself. A lark spiraled skyward from the meadow on the other side of the hill, singing joyously, but she was in no mood to sing back to it. She tried to pick some of the mud off her dress, but the outer layer had already cracked off during the night, and the rest had soaked right into the material, and hardened.

Presently she stood up. "You can stay here all day if

you like," she announced stiffly, "but I'm going down the hill and see if I can find a stream to wash in. Perhaps you'll be human again when I get back." And she started down the hill.

James roused himself instantly at this. He turned his head, fixed her with a masterful stare, and pointed back at the tree. "You stay right there!" he commanded quietly.

Lark looked at him with some astonishment. "Yes, James," she said, and obeyed him with a new and very great respect in her heart. It was one thing for her to decide not to manage him any more, and quite another for him to put his own foot down so firmly. She loved him, she decided, more than ever.

James, feeling slightly foolish over it all, looked at her ruefully and tried to decide whether to try to explain things, but he never had a chance to make up his mind. For at that moment the sound of a small but energetic battle erupted near the foot of the hill.

James completely forgot his moral dilemma. Through the trees he could see clearly enough that a small number of Royalists were fighting against about twice as many Roundhead soldiers, and nothing else mattered for the moment. "You stay right there!" he barked at Lark, and rushed down the hill and into battle—precisely as she had feared he would.

She promptly disobeyed him. Did he think for one moment that she would just *sit* there while he got killed? Not likely! Although her heart was positively flapping with fright, she crept cautiously down the hill in James's footsteps, promising herself only that she would stay a safe distance away because it would upset James and perhaps distract him if he were to see her. But her idea of a safe distance was hardly further than the nearest tree, where she armed herself with a stout stick and a stone the size of her fist, and lurked anxiously. If James should need help, she would do what she could—though she was not at all sure how much help she could be.

James was already in the fight, his eyes glittering. Here, at least, was a clear-cut issue. The Roundheads were attacking English Royalists, not Scots, and they badly outnumbered them. Right in front of James a Royalist was trying to cope with two Roundheads at once. James attacked the nearest with fierce joy, his dagger now in his left hand, and his right curled lovingly around the sword which he had already acquired from a now unconscious Roundhead before Lark got there.

It was his first real fight, but he had no sense of fear. He was seized with the superhuman skill and strength that often comes to people who are fighting for what they believe to be a righteous cause. He disarmed the second soldier in seconds, and allowed his blade to continue in a thrust straight for the heart. And then, in the last split second, he deflected his blade and ran the man through the shoulder instead. He hadn't intended to. But it seemed that even stronger than rage was his instinct not to kill if disabling would do as well. James, considerably astonished at himself, paused for an instant to make sure that the man would not hold a sword for some time to come. Then, with a shrug, he looked for a new Roundhead to conquer.

From behind her tree—or at least partly behind it—Lark watched with a chalky face. "Please, God!" she murmured over and over. "Oh, God, *please!*" James would surely be killed against such odds, and— "Oh, God, *please!*" He was deeper into the skirmish now, so that she couldn't see him very well. The other Royalists seemed much too occupied even to notice the addition of James. And it occurred to Lark that with things as confused as they were, and James being dressed in Roundhead clothes and with cropped hair, the Royalists might take him for an enemy, so that he might end up fighting both sides at once.

And then, just as Lark really thought she couldn't bear it an instant longer, there were new sounds from the trees beyond the clearing. She took her eyes off James for just one second. When she looked back, the soldier whom he had disabled was rising, his sword in his left hand, about to plunge it into James's back.

"Behind you, James!" screamed Lark with all her strength. "Look out behind you!"

15
James's Hole

James heard. He twisted to one side just an instant too late. And as a reinforcement of Royalist soldiers charged into the clearing, James fell. Lark saw it clearly . . . and then she didn't see anything else for a minute or two because a kind of mist closed in, and she was sick and dizzy, and her legs would no longer hold her up. James was dead. Lark whimpered like a hurt puppy, and sank shivering into a small huddle behind the tree.

But only for a moment. Then she was stumbling through the undergrowth toward the clearing, sobbing and calling out to the Royalists in a muffled voice that they could not possibly have heard over the renewed din of their skirmish. It was an extremely brief skirmish. By the time Lark reached the clearing, the Royalists were vanishing again on the other side, taking, it appeared, their own dead and all of the wounded with them. Lark gave one last shrill call after them, but with no effect. They were clearly in a great hurry, and in a moment she couldn't even hear them any longer.

Three or four still figures still lay in the clearing, and among them was the lean brown one of James—now reddened considerably about the middle. Lark had never been able to bear the sight of anyone's blood except her own, and not much of that; but now she knelt beside James without a thought for her own squeamishness. Tears poured down her face and dripped off her chin, but she had stopped sobbing because it was necessary to find out whether James might still be alive after all, and she could not hear his heart beat over her own noise.

But it was going to be difficult to hear his heart anyway, for he was lying on his face, and Lark was afraid to move him. Instead, she took his outflung arm and felt awkwardly at the wrist with her small fingers. At first she could feel nothing at all and then, suddenly, she found the right place, and there was a pulse that really seemed surprisingly strong. He was alive!

Lark stopped crying altogether and became quite calm. She had to. James's life might depend on her calmness.

The wound was low at the back of his ribs, and she studied the spreading patch of red on his jerkin for a moment, and then eased the dagger out of his left hand. For surely the logical thing to do first was to stop the bleeding.

Carefully she ripped through the seam of his jerkin and pulled at his shirt until she could see what seemed to her a perfectly huge and deep cut, bleeding steadily. Lark turned a little whiter than she was before, and began muttering to God under her breath. She did not feel capable of dealing with this without His help.

Perhaps God began telling her what to do directly, or perhaps He helped her mind to work with unusual clarity and intelligence. At any rate, Lark swiftly hacked and tore her petticoat until she had cut off a wide strip from the bottom edge. She looked at it doubtfully. It was quite caked with mud, and although no one had ever suggested to her that dirt was bad for wounds, she doubted that it was really *good* for them. She laid it down, fetched her bag from where it had dropped when the Roundhead grabbed her, and tore a strip from her nightgown instead. Even this might be cleaner, but at least there was no caked mud on it.

She folded it into a thick compress and pressed it firmly upon the cut, her brows knit with anxiety. She hoped this was right. If not, she did not at all know what else to do. The linen was staining around the edges, but then presently the red seemed to spread more slowly. Encouraged, Lark rearranged her legs in a more comfortable position and prepared to stay there for days if necessary.

Presently James stirred. His eyelids flickered and then closed again, and he frowned and sighed.

"James!" whispered Lark, the tears beginning to flood downward again. "Oh, James!"

James opened his eyes for an instant without really seeing anything. "Wurramarra?" he mumbled groggily. He tried to move, winced, and decided hazily that something was biting his back. "Wuzzabagare?" he demanded, moving his arm in a feeble and irritated effort to brush whatever it was away.

Lark promptly stopped crying again. "Stop that!" she commanded briskly. "Hold still, James Trelawney; do you hear me?"

Her imperious tone penetrated the fog of James's mind. He relaxed again and tried to collect his thoughts. Roundheads . . . a fight . . . Lark . . . Oh yes. And her shriek of warning, and then the pain in his ribs . . . and had there been a blow on his head, too? He rather thought so. Yes, he could remember now, and it was beginning to hurt outrageously just over his left ear. But what had happened next? He blinked and peered at the little he could see with one eye practically buried in the grass.

"Lark?" he managed to say, and tried to look over his own shoulder and down his back.

"Hold still!" repeated Lark worriedly. "Are you all right, James? Does it hurt very much? You don't think you're dying, do you?"

James considered the question for a moment, and then decided that he wasn't. "No," he said with some difficulty. "Warra you doing, Lark?"

"You've got a hole in you, and I'm keeping the blood from all running out," she told him with masterful simplicity. "If I go on holding it, will it stop, or should I be doing something else to close up the hole?"

James indicated weakly that she was doubtlessly doing the best thing, and then closed his eyes again and tried to clear his head. It felt very muddled, and he didn't think he was going to be able to offer her much intelligent advice. But Lark could see that this was the case, and she braced herself to carry on alone.

Time passed. The sun was high now, and it was getting

hot. But at last, when Lark ventured to lift the pad for a moment, the bleeding seemed to have stopped.

"How do you feel now, James?" she asked, bending closer to his head. "I think I might try to tie a pad on you with another strip of my nightgown to hold it, and then I was wondering if I could help you crawl as far as the stream. I do think you ought to have a drink, and perhaps I could wash your wound, and anyway, you should be out of the sun where it's cooler."

James thought he could manage this, and even raised himself enough for her to pass the strip of linen under and around him. Then the two of them set out on the long hard trip of twenty years or so to the coolness of the shaded stream bank.

Lark, fussing like a grandmother, gave him water to drink from her cupped hands—which was harder than it sounded, and took a great many tries. Then she washed out the strip of petticoat and laid it, cold and wet from the stream, across the large lump on his head.

James sighed a little as the coolness of shade and water began to penetrate. He indicated to the hovering Lark that yes he did think he could sleep a little, and closed his eyes. He shouldn't, of course; he could not afford to be an invalid just now. But after just a short nap he would be himself again. It wasn't his wound that was really bothering him. He felt sure that was really quite minor, in spite of Lark's alarm. But if only his head would stop aching! Why was it, he wondered sleepily, that a pain in the head seemed so much worse than a pain somewhere else? One could be a bit detached about a leg or arm or even a back, but a person lived in his head, didn't he? Perhaps the soul as well as the mind lived there but James wasn't sure. Presently he couldn't quite remember what it was he wasn't sure about. Things seemed to elude him. He slept.

When he awoke, his head still ached, but it no longer felt as if it were about to shatter into a dozen pieces. And although his wound hurt, it was not at all unbearable. James really had no notion whether it was a bad wound or not. He stirred a little, and became aware that his head was resting on what seemed to be Lark's bag, or perhaps her cloak, and that he was extremely warm. Possibly it was due to the fact that it was a hot day even under the trees, and he was covered besides with his own cloak. Lark must have gone back and collected the various things left on top of the hill.

He opened his eyes rather quickly, for it occurred to him that he wasn't hearing any sounds that might be Lark, and if anything—His eyes fell directly upon her small smudgy face and round eyes staring at him as intently as a kitten watching a mousehole. She gave a great sigh and a wavering smile.

James returned the smile, but then shut his eyes again for a minute, because he had a good deal of thinking to do. Once again a new element had entered their situation, causing all of the bits and pieces to fall into a new pattern. He considered it gloomily. Whatever else, it was clear that poor Lark would have to take on a good deal more of the work and responsibility, for James as well as herself. He wondered how far he could travel, and if . . .

An astonishing fact occurred to him. He was free—for the present, anyway—from his horrible dilemma! He no longer had to decide whether to join King Charles's army, because it was out of the question now. He had fought his battle. Moreover, it had been a clear choice, where he had been sure of his duty. He had helped English Royalists, and his conscience was quite clear. Since it would no doubt be a while before he was fit to fight again, he could devote his attention to getting Lark to safety in the meantime.

He opened his eyes, feeling better already. "What happened, anyway?" he asked. "I mean, after I got hit on the head?"

Lark shook her head. "I'm not sure. It was all so fast and muddled. But some other Royalists came, and I expect they thought you were a dead Roundhead, because they left you there. And nobody heard me shouting at them. They were in an awful hurry!"

James pondered this for some time, trying to figure it out. The little group of Cavaliers had likely been an advance scouting party for King Charles and his Scots, but everything else seemed to be uncertain. At any rate, it did not seem probable that the entire army—for either side—would be marching through this out-of-the-way wooded valley. There would be no point in it.

James resigned himself to probably never knowing exactly what had happened or why, or even whether his help had been of any real importance. He sighed and sat up carefully, wincing just a trifle, for both his head and back objected to this.

"I'm all right," he said when Lark protested. "I'm tougher than you think. Anyway, I think we'd better move on as soon as possible." He eyed the sun, which was only halfway down the sky.

"Indeed we shouldn't!" Lark said with indignation. "You're wounded, James! You mustn't move at all!"

James shook his head vigorously and immediately regretted it. "Indeed we must!" he retorted, and added the shrewdest argument he could have used. "It's for my sake, too, Lark. We must try to find a house where they'll take us in. You're a wonderful nurse, but there's a limit to what you can do with just water and bits of nightgown, you know." He swallowed and tried to look strong and healthy. "I feel quite good now, so why don't we get started soon, and perhaps we'll find a house before dark."

Lark gave in against her instinct. "Well . . ." she said doubtfully, and eyed him with misgiving. He looked very pale. But when he had moved around a little, and his wound had not started to bleed again, and he insisted that he felt fine, she reluctantly agreed to start.

16
Lark in Command

Late afternoon of the next day found Lark stumbling blindly and despairingly behind James through a tangle of bracken, with no house or human in sight. James was stumbling even more. His face was at hot and red as a stove, and his wits seemed to be wandering, but he would not stop. He had it in his mind that he must find someone to take care of Lark, and he kept muttering about it. But Lark was quite sure that they were going in spirals, further and further into the wild mountains of Wales.

"Please, James," she begged again. "Please let's stop! You need to rest."

James plowed mulishly on, right up a woody hill that couldn't possibly hold a human being. Lark choked back a sob and followed helplessly. They had found some water that day, which James had drunk greedily, but he seemed not even to notice that they had not eaten. He was going to go on and on, deeper into the mountains, until he just fell down and died; and there was nothing she could do about it.

James reached a clear place near the top of the hill where the slope fell away steeply ahead of him. He tottered for a minute, and if Lark had not dropped her bag and grabbed at him, he would have fallen headlong down it.

"Please, James!" she panted.

James looked at her blankly and allowed himself to lean against a tree. "Should be houses," he muttered hoarsely. "Houses somewhere. Don't worry, Lark; I'll take care of you." He closed his eyes for a moment, and then tried to straighten up and go on.

Lark grabbed his arm with sudden fury. Enough of being sweet and tactful! This was no time, she realized suddenly, for gentle nudges at the tiller. If the captain was wounded and delirious, it was time to rap his knuckles until he let go, and take over the steering altogether.

"You sit down this minute, James Trelawney!" she exploded so threateningly that James regarded her with bewildered eyes and obeyed. His knees sagged, he slid slowly down the tree trunk, and then gently rolled over on the ground; he was quite unconscious.

Lark looked at him in horror. She stared around wildly at the desolate scene, barren even of water. She put her hand on his burning face and was more frightened than ever. What could she do? She had not the least idea. His wound wasn't bleeding, and although she had heard vaguely that wounds could kill people in other ways than bleeding, she had no notion what those ways were or what to do about it. She couldn't even go for help, for James might wander off in his delirium.

Lark wrapped both cloaks around his still figure, put her nightgown under his head, and couldn't think of anything else. Then, quite at her wits end, she dropped to the ground beside him and wept wildly. Nothing in her life had ever been as bad as this; not when Father was wounded, or when Uncle Jeremiah stole her, or even yesterday when James had fallen in the battle. She cried until her head felt swollen to twice its size, and ached, and she simply hadn't the strength to cry any more.

Then she lay numbly, with her hand in James's hot one, not able to think, or even to pray. She ought to pray, no doubt, but she couldn't. She was a little afraid to, for one thing, in case God might turn out to be Uncle Jeremiah's. Besides, this wasn't the same as yesterday, when there was something that needed doing at once, and her mind was alert and ready to receive any suggestions God might offer. This was different. Lark felt that it would take a huge miracle to help James now, and she was afraid to pray for it, because if her prayer was not answered her last hope would be gone, and her faith as well.

But as she lay huddled on the ground, drained and limp, something in her seemed to rise slowly on a wave of love for James, and a willingness to do anything at all for him, and a wish for wisdom so that she might know what to do. She did not know that she was praying; she had thought that prayer came in words, formally addressed to God. Presently she began to feel a sense of calm and new strength.

She raised her swollen face and looked at James again.

His burning hand stirred feebly in hers, and he muttered something about having to take care of her—in just a minute now. Lark leaned over him.

"James!" she said urgently. "James, can you hear me?"

James opened his eyes briefly, and they were rational. "Lark?" he said painfully through swollen and cracked lips. "Sorry, Lark, I—I'm not being very helpful. I'll—"

"Listen, James!" said Lark. "You mustn't try to move now. Do you hear? You *must* stay right here. I'm going to go look around a little to see if I can find a house or some water. Do you understand, James? Don't move, or I might not be able to find you again. Will you remember?"

In the midst of his fever, James realized that he had to leave everything to Lark now. It was her right, and the only hope for either of them. He nodded weakly, and even managed the ghost of a grin. "I couldn't—go far," he muttered, and wanted to add something about Lark finding her way back; but it was too much effort, and anyway, she seemed to know what she was doing.

He watched through half-opened eyes while she rummaged in her bag for the two sets of white collar and cap. She had not worn them since the inn at Shrewsbury, first because they would show more in the dark, and then because of the mud, and finally because there had been too many other things to think about. She stuck them in the front of her bodice for convenience, took off her shoes and stockings, and looked carefully for a tall and easily climbed tree. If she tied the white collars and caps to branches, then surely they would show up enough to guide her back, in case she should get confused. The sun would be up for hours yet, for it was still August and the days were long.

She marched up to the tree she had picked and paused, fighting off a slight feeling of dizziness. It was, she reminded herself, only because she hadn't eaten for quite a long time. Nothing to get dizzy about, really. Lots of people went for a long time without eating, and still managed to do things. Besides, she had to. There was no one else. With a deep breath, she reached for the lowest branch and began climbing, slowly but steadily, being very careful because if she should fall, then James would be quite helpless.

Presently she found a place where she could walk out on a branch while holding to the one above, and there she tied the first cap as far out as she could reach. It made a splendid spot of white in all the brown and tawny and green. Encouraged, she climbed higher and did the same thing on the other side of the tree.

From this branch, she could see down the hill to what seemed to be a fair-sized valley. Surely a valley should have water at least, and perhaps people? She craned her neck hopefully. But there were too many trees in the way, and the shoulder of the hill besides. With a sigh—for she really was feeling terribly tired—she made her way higher in the tree.

And then . . . surely there was something moving down there? Lark's heart began thumping with hope that scarcely dared to exist. At the risk of losing her balance altogether, she did squirrel-like things until at last, through the leaves, she saw a caravan of brightly painted wagons just moving into the valley.

Gypsies! She would have been delighted even to find Roundheads or bandits. But Gypsies were kind, as she well knew. Hastily tying a collar to the branch above her, Lark slid down the tree, fastened the other collar on the lowest branch, and turned to James. But he was unconscious again.

There was no time to rouse him. Lark set off down the hill toward the now-invisible caravan at a suicidal pace. She scarcely dared hope that it might be Psammis's tribe; she would settle for any humans at all!

She plunged ahead, remembering that they had been just in line with the sun, and keeping to that direction. At a less desperate time she would have gone around steep places and slides of scree, but not now. Branches lashed across her face and tore the sturdy homespun of her skirt as she went. In steep places she sometimes went too fast for her feet, and fell. Once she rolled all the way down a slide, and another time she landed on her wrist so painfully that all she could do for a moment was to hold it, gasping, while pain shot up her arm like knives, and her stomach churned. Then she stumbled to her feet again and went on.

Gradually the slope became less steep, and after some time she found herself on more open ground where she could once again see the wagons. There were even figures walking along beside them. Lark picked up speed and found breath to call. "Help! Wait! Please!"

Someone turned. Someone else pointed. Her feet moving mechanically now, Lark labored on, staring through blurred eyes. Could that be a small round figure in the back of the yellow wagon? And the massive bearded man coming from the front of the caravan . . .

"Psammis!" she bleated. "Psammis! Sheba!"

And then she was surrounded by familiar faces, then she was sobbing and gasping in the ample strength of

Sheba's arms. "James—help—" she managed, and then had no more breath.

"Quiet, small Gorgio; breathe deeply, then tell us," commanded Sheba. And in a minute Lark was able to talk.

"James—he's hurt—up on the hill. He's sick and out of his wits, and I think he's— Please help him, please! If you don't, he—" She couldn't finish. Instead she smeared sudden tears across her face with the back of her hand and stared at them pleadingly, a most thoroughly filthy and wretched small person, even by Gypsy standards.

"Where?" asked Psammis simply.

Lark pointed up the hill, where two of her four spots of white could be seen amid green foliage. "There," she said, equally brief.

"Come," said Psammis to Neco and a villainous-looking Gypsy named Otho. "We will find him," he told Lark. "You need not come."

"Yes," said Lark firmly. "I do need."

Sheba, looking at her, nodded. "She and I will come," she said.

Psammis regarded Lark doubtfully, but as usual he took Sheba's advice and said no more, but began leading the way back up the hill.

It was even longer going back than Lark remembered. She labored on, behind Neco and in front of Sheba, determined to make it on her own. And now that she had found help—a true miracle, and a large one—she began to worry for fear that James might after all have wandered off and become lost.

Psammis, with the Gypsy gift for following trails, had no trouble at all tracing the wild and broken line of Lark's descent. But once in a while he looked at a particularly steep and reckless bit, and turned around to eye her wonderingly. Clearly this child had far more in her than Psammis ever imagined.

But Lark was finding it very hard going. Her wrist throbbed and hurt badly. Often she stumbled, and once would have fallen flat but that Sheba suddenly put a firm brown hand on her shoulder. The hand did more than steady her; it somehow gave her strength. Lark felt it in a swift surge and wondered whether it was Gypsy magic or some particular healing gift of Sheba's. She turned her head with new hope. "Can you do that for James?" she asked breathlessly.

Sheba smiled enigmatically and did not answer, but Lark found the rest of her climb easier in spirit as well as body.

James was still there! He was also looking, if possible, worse than ever. Lark gave a small squeak of relief and dismay combined. And then she stood still while Sheba crossed swiftly and knelt down beside him. She put her hands on each side of his face, across his temples and over his head, looking grave as she felt the heat of his fever. She kept her hands there a long moment, and Lark did not know whether she was doing magic or just learning somehow what was wrong with James and how sick he was. She listened to his heart, she felt his wrists, and put her hands at the sides of his ribs. Then she turned to Psammis. "We will take him down on a litter," she said.

The three men made one swiftly, with long poles and the cloaks. James opened his eyes as they bent over him, and frowned. He knew his wits were wandering, and it was a great annoyance to him. Didn't he have enough real things to worry about without seeing imaginary ones besides? Last time it had been his father that he had seen, and before that the Roundheads at the Blue Dolphin, and now it was the Gypsies. To make it worse, he could even hear them. Most confusing of all, he could also see and hear Lark, but since she didn't look any more real than the Gypsies, how was he to know whether she was really there or not?

"Lark?" he asked rather crossly.

She—or his illusion of her—came over and knelt beside him and took his hand. James, still not sure if she was real, felt that he wanted to explain his difficulty to her, if she *was* there, that is. But it seemed very complicated.

"Ha—" he said with great effort. "Hallu—cin—ations," he managed, and closed his eyes again, feeling that he had explained everything in a most scientific way. And although he was dimly aware of being lifted and carried gently down the hill, he thought that he was now merely extraordinarily dizzy in addition to everything else.

The one comforting thing was that Lark's hand seemed to be near: sometimes holding his, sometimes touching him when he called to be sure she was there. He did hope she was all right . . . She kept saying she was . . . He must get better as soon as possible in order to make sure . . .

Lark stayed on her feet until they were back at the caravan and Sheba vanished with James into the yellow wagon. Then, since there was no longer a great need for her to stay conscious, she quietly collapsed.

17

The Yellow Wagon

When James was again able to tell what was really happening from what wasn't, he found that he was with the Gypsies again. This confused him so much that he went back to sleep for a whole day.

By the time he was able to take an intelligent interest in things, he was already convalescing, and consequently inclined to be both irritable and unreasonable. He was aggrieved to find that he had somehow lost more than a week, and that it was now September. He demanded to know *what* had been going on, and whether the expected battle *had* taken place, and why no one ever *told* him anything.

Lark regarded him doubtfully. He looked very pale and thin on the pallet in the back of the yellow wagon, and not up to much excitement. Moreover, Sheba had particularly warned Lark not to upset him in any way, and

Sheba had become very possessive and motherly toward James while she was saving his life.

"Well?" demanded James, beginning to look upset.

Lark decided she had better tell him. "Well—yes," she admitted, trying to sound as cheerful as possible about it. "The battle was at Worcester three days ago. We heard that the English Royalists and the Highlanders fought splendidly, and if the Lowland troops hadn't gone and refused to fight, mostly, why King Charles might not have—uh—well, lost the battle."

It was a severe blow, even though James had expected it. He put a hand over his eyes. "Badly?" His voice was muffled.

"Well, yes," Lark admitted. It was getting harder to be cheerful. "But they do say King Charles got away," she told him soothingly.

James did not look soothed. "Got away?" he echoed, digesting this. "*Got away!* You mean he hasn't got any army at all any more? It's all wiped out?"

He was looking alarmingly excited. "Shhh," said Lark hastily. "Don't upset yourself, James! Anyway, it isn't *all* wiped out. Quite a lot of Cavaliers and Scots got away, and I know they haven't all been caught, because the Roundheads are still hunting for them. They even searched us once, and Sheba had to put something on your face to make it come out all over with spots, so they thought it was a horrible disease, and the Hand of God, and they rode away in a hurry just in case it got on them, too." She chuckled.

James was not amused. "I'm glad you think it's funny!" he snarled. "It's merely the end of everything we believed in and fought for, and Cromwell will take over everything now! I warrant you'll laugh pretty hard when your uncle takes you back again for good, won't you?"

Lark stared at him unbelievingly, her feelings seriously wounded. She tried to remind herself that he had been very ill and was not himself, and had had a very hard time. But then, she had had a hard time, too, and in some ways harder than James. After all, he had been more or less peacefully unconscious all the time she had been climbing trees and falling down mountains and cracking her wrist for his sake, and all the days since when she had been half crazy with fear that he would die, and even these last days when they had actually *heard* the sounds of the battle, and she had had that to worry about, too. She choked back an angry retort, and then bit her lip to keep it from quivering, and sat in silence for a moment trying to control herself.

"I'm s-sorry," she said at last in a small and subdued voice, but with a new kind of dignity. "I think you'd b-better get some sleep, James."

James immediately perceived that he had been a beast and also that this was no way to prepare a girl for wanting to marry him when she grew up. This last thought surprised him a trifle. He had not known it was in his mind before now. But once he thought about it, he saw that it was perfectly natural and inevitable, and altogether the cleverest idea he had ever had.

"I'm a beast," he said remorsefully. "Forgive me, Lark. Are you all right? Why is your arm all bandaged like that?"

"I cracked it or something—uh—coming down a hill," replied Lark, immediately mollified. She gave him a dazzling smile. "Oh, James, I'm sorry if I annoyed you, but I was trying *not* to upset you with bad news; and anyway I'm so glad you're going to get well that I haven't got much sadness left for the battle. I was *so* scared you were going to die!"

They looked at each other with some satisfaction. James was thinking that Lark really was devoted to him, and perhaps he had not, after all, spoiled his plan to marry her some day. Lark was way ahead of him. She was thinking that this was splendid practice in handling her husband-to-be in his more difficult moments.

But before they could say any more, Sheba appeared, took one look at James, shooed Lark out, and ordered her patient to compose his mind at once and go to sleep.

James, of course, did nothing of the sort. Instead, he lay and fretted about what was likely to happen to England, the Royalists, King Charles, his parents, and, most particularly, his Lark. None of it looked at all heartening. And he was in the frame of mind where he felt himself personally responsible for everything that had happened or might happen. He had just about concluded that the battle had been lost for the lack of just one more soldier (himself) on the side of Charles, and was going on to decide that somehow he would doubtless manage to lead Lark right back into the arms of Uncle Jeremiah, when Sheba looked in on him again.

She saw at once that he was working himself into another fever, and being a very wise woman, she decided that he had better get things off his chest. So she fetched Lark back and told them to go ahead and be as upset as they liked until James's hot broth was ready.

James forgot about Lark needing to be protected from too much knowledge and worry. Somehow she had become his comrade, someone to share things with. He told her everything that was distressing him, especially the bit about how to reach his parents and then get over to France to find hers.

"The Roundheads will be six times as thick and suspicious and nosy now," he concluded. "Especially in Devon, which is strongly Royalist. For all I know, my parents have already been turned out of their home. And on top of it all, here I am as weak as a kitten, and you with a broken arm, and both of us with practically no money left."

Lark thought about it for a minute or two. There was a new kind of serenity about her, which James found intriguing. "My arm isn't broken," she pointed out presently. "It didn't have to be set or anything. And I don't think we ought to worry about the other things yet, because there isn't anything we can *do* right now, is there, except get well. And when there is, I dare say you'll think of it," she went on trustingly. "You always do."

Somehow James found himself comforted and reassured by her confidence in him.

As a matter of fact, Lark's new confidence wasn't entirely in James. During the worst times, after he had been wounded, she hadn't been able to lean on him at all. She had been forced to depend on herself and God, and as a consequence she had made some most interesting discoveries.

God, she had decided, wasn't an irascible old fellow with a thunderbolt in one hand, at all. He was a sort of Power that was always right there, like air. And prayer wasn't telling God what to do, as Uncle Jeremiah seemed to think. It was a wordless sort of thinking that could go on in the back of one's mind all the time, like breathing air. And then in special emergencies it was like a silent yell for help. Lark had yelled for help that day on the mountain, and the help had come. She thought it very kind of God to arrange a special miracle, one way or another, and she had a brand new confidence in Him.

She put in a special thought about all their various problems, left the back of her mind open to any hints that God might choose to send disguised as a bright idea, and then left all the details to Him.

She left James to his nap and got down to walk along with the caravan—always close to the yellow wagon, in case James should need anything.

She was the first thing James saw when he awoke and let his fancy drift out through the wagon doorway. He smiled to himself at the faithful small figure, and then looked again. He had been remembering an enchanting small girl by the side of a river, who had pushed him and the lout off the bank and then later spread out her hair to dry and calmly announced that she was going to Scotland. Only that morning he had been thinking that he would marry her when she grew up. Now it occurred to him that it might not be as long as he had thought. Lark was growing up, practically under his eyes. She didn't even look about ten years old any longer. Her face was thinner, for one thing. And she had a different expression, for another. James decided with satisfaction that perhaps he could request her hand in marriage almost as soon as he found her parents and restored her to them. They would probably be feeling quite kindly toward him, too. With these pleasant thoughts, James slept once more.

By the next day he was able to worry more actively about the unknown fate of King Charles, and also (in between worrying) to remember brief snatches of the days he had lost.

"I think I do remember a little about Roundheads searching," he told Lark. "I thought it was a dream. My face was hot and itched horribly, and I remember hearing some child roaring and howling like all the lions in the Tower of London put together."

"That was Berry being spanked," Lark told him, looking amused. "She decided she wasn't going to let the Roundheads go past her into the wagon, and when one of them tried, she bit him. And no one ever told the Roundhead that no one was allowed to lay a finger on Berry, so he did. Hard. You never saw anybody so astonished and furious in your life. She was so mad that when he finished spanking her and gave her to Sheba, she bit Sheba too, and got another spanking; and now she gets them whenever she needs them."

"Well!" James digested this slowly. "I'm surprised there wasn't knife play when a Gorgio dared hit a Romany child."

Lark leaned over and whispered. "I think everyone in the tribe thought it was good for her," she whispered. "But Bracken's the only one that says so out loud."

James grinned and kept his opinion to himself. Then he frowned. "Where are we?" he wanted to know. "Where are we heading? Are there any plans? Has anyone heard anything of the King? We've got to get me well as fast as we can, Lark, because we're a danger to the tribe every minute we're here."

"Well, you *can't* leave for a while yet, however much you want to," Lark said complacently. (She and Sheba had an unspoken agreement that they would cheerfully risk all sorts of other lives for James's.) "Anyhow, I don't think they'd let you just *go*. Not now. You've been adopted. Sheba says she gave you life as much as your real mother did, and that makes you her son."

Willow stuck her head in the wagon door at this point, and batted her eyelashes at James, partly to tease Lark and partly because he *was* a most attractive young man. "And now we are going to take you home, Adopted Brother," she announced in a voice that was anything but sisterly. "We might as well; we have nowhere else in particular to go, and the southern counties are best in winter. Besides, when we get there, we'll camp as long as we like on your land, won't we?"

"Certainly," agreed James promptly, that being the very least he could do. "For as long as I or my heirs own it . . . that is, if we own it at all any more," he added glumly. "I expect the Roundheads will be turning even more Royalists out of their homes than ever, now."

Willow ignored this awful possibility. She tossed her dark head so that the golden hoops in her ears swung, and slitted her eyes. "When we are there, I shall amuse all your friends and family," she decided. "I shall show them some Gypsy tricks, and they will be very much impressed, I promise you." She smiled dazzlingly at James, expecting him to say that that would be very nice.

Instead, he stretched his lips across his teeth at her in what really could not at all be called a smile. "Oh, no, you won't!" he declared a trifle grimly.

Willow looked put-upon. "But I'm *very* good at them!" she bragged, unable to understand James's narrow-minded attitude. "You ought to see me!" She looked at Lark speculatively.

But Lark had heard enough to draw some very accurate conclusions about the nature of these tricks. She laughed and shook her head.

Willow moped, disappointed. Gorgios were always taking the fun out of things.

18
A Manor in Devon

The Gypsy caravan moved along lanes and byways down past Bristol and into Devon through a most upset countryside. Things still seethed with the last battle of a lost cause, with rampant Roundheads hunting Royalists, Scots, and most particularly one Charles Stewart. Rumors flew. The King was captured; he had fled back to Scotland; he was in hiding; he was dead and secretly buried.

But the Romany were not part of that world. They moved in a dimension of their own, and James and Lark with them. Only once or twice did the outside world break in, in the form of soldiers wanting to search the wagons. But these invasions were hardly more than a gesture, since no one seriously supposed that Gypsies would risk their own necks and forfeit all those rewards for any Gorgio. And if two of the ragged, dirty, earringed Gypsies had rather lighter hair than most of them, no one ever bothered to look twice.

By the time they reached Devon, James was very nearly his old self again. He claimed it was the air and the good red soil of his own country that did it.

"It's a well-known scientific fact," he told Lark, "that just returning to the place of your birth can cure the most remarkable number of ailments."

Lark eyed him sideways. She was developing a rather scientific mind of her own, and it occurred to her that there might be other factors at work.

"Sheba said days ago that you'd suddenly start feeling much better about now," she reminded him. "Besides, the sun's just come out after all those days of rain, so that I feel especially well myself; and I'm not returning to my place of birth. I was never in Devon before in my life."

James grinned down at her, quite admiring her practical nature. "But you see, you have an illogical female mind," he teased her, wagging his head solemnly.

"I see," Lark said thoughtfully. "Then men's minds are logical?"

James nodded, curious to hear what would come next.

"And it was men, of course, who figured out about men being the logical ones?"

Another nod.

"Like the men who are kings, and logically try to make their people like them by bringing in a foreign army to invade," Lark went on hastily, "and the men who invented Puritanism—"

"Help!" said James weakly. "Don't start on Puritanism! I give up! . . . I can hardly wait for you to meet my mother," he added with anticipation. "Excuse me for a few minutes, Lark. I know the man who owns that farm."

He left the caravan and reappeared some time later, looking pleased. "The King still hasn't been caught," he reported. "At least it's pretty sure he hasn't."

This had been going on ever since they got into Devon, for James had done a great deal of messenger work here before branching into other counties. Now there was hardly a Royalist home where he wasn't known—even in Puritan brown or in Gypsy rags. As a result, he was able to pick up quite a lot of information as they headed south and west.

There was a very healthy underground system in play here in the West Country for getting hunted Royalists out of the country and across the Channel. Even though ports and harbors were well watched, fishing boats managed to leave every day from some secluded cove or another, bearing refugees.

"Actually, it's been going on in a way for a long time," James explained to Lark. "People get put out of their homes, for instance, so that they go into exile in France—like your parents. Only Cromwell never minded before. He said it was good riddance, so long as they didn't take too much with them. Now it's different, because he wants to hang every supporter of Charles he can catch. I expect we'll have to wait for a while to cross, Lark," he added. "You see, the ones whose lives are in danger have first rights."

Lark nodded, not at all distressed. She wanted very much to see her parents again, of course, but she did not want to be separated from James. He had never said anything about what was to happen after he found her family and restored her to them, and she was a little reluctant to mention it, because it might sound like a hint. It was quite important, Lark felt, that James should think it all his own idea to marry her—when he got around to thinking of it at all, she added to herself with a sigh. She really did want things understood, if possible, before having to be separated from him for a long time, when other girls might have ideas about James, themselves.

"It might take quite a while to find out where Mother and Father are," she suggested. "How will we go about it, James?"

"Oh, there are several possibilities," murmured James absently. It vaguely occurred to him that he had not yet got around to finding out their names, but that didn't seem important at the moment. "There are communications between the Royalists here and in exile. My parents might possibly know. Or there's that 'fine gentleman' we keep hearing about, who comes over from France in his private boat and takes Royalists back with him. He might know, and at the very least he could carry messages for us, and start inquiring."

He left her again to pay another visit and pick up another thread in the trail he was following. It was an elderly gentleman, he learned, though some said he was a young man in disguise. He hid his boat in some cove or on one of the rivers, and came further upstream in a dory, usually. But no one seemed to know any more, or how to get in touch with him. It was not much to go on—but on the other hand, this was Devon, and there was time.

James felt more and more optimistic the closer he got to his home.

Early on a misty mid-September day, a tribe of Gypsies turned off a Devon road into a green meadow, protected with trees, and with a stream running along one side. They proceeded to make camp just as if they had been personally invited to stay there—which, as a matter of fact, was the case. Presently two very dirty Gypsies detached themselves from the others and went hand in hand through a wood, across another field, past stables and garden, and up to a gray stone manor house. There they paused a moment, looked down at themselves, chuckled, and then went to the kitchen door rather than the front entrance.

"For one thing, it's closer," observed James with amusement, "and for another, I shouldn't think anything like us has ever gone in at the front door yet, so why should we start now?"

With Lark's hand firmly in his, he walked jauntily up to the kitchen door and stuck his head into the upper half, which stood open. The serving maid, who happened to look up from the oaken sideboard at that moment, gave a small shriek of alarm, looked around for help, and then prepared to stand and give battle.

"Go away!" she squeaked. "Ee can't come in here, ee nasty dirty thieving Gypsies! Oi'll have t'coachman on ee, so oi will!"

"Don't be silly, Joan," said James, laughing. "Look hard and you'll know me. Where are Mother and Father?"

"Awp?" said Joan, peering at him doubtfully, and seeming more distressed than ever at finding James's familiar face behind the dirt. "Master, Mistress!" she squealed, running through the inner door and along the hallway. "Come quick!"

When Sir William and Lady Trelawney arrived in their kitchen, escorted by the fluttering Joan, James had made himself and Lark quite at home, and was just helping them to a large slice of ham from the spit.

"Mercy!" said his mother, and was then enveloped in a highly unwashed hug that left her breathless. James hugged his father too, and the three of them looked at one another happily for an instant. All of them, being bred and trained in self-control, recovered it at once.

"Well, my dear," observed Lady Trelawney, "I must confess that I might not have recognized you immediately in a crowd. Hadn't you better introduce me to your friend?"

"Oh, I *am* sorry!" James exclaimed, and turned to Lark. "This is Lark—uh—"

"Elizabeth Lennox, Lark for short," supplied Lark, curtseying.

Lady Trelawney perceived at once from the manners and accent that Lark was a member of their own aristocratic class. It took her at least three seconds longer to see that there was a very stong attachment indeed between little Mistress Lennox and James. After that, it was a mere matter of one question to establish—satisfyingly—that Lark's parents were Lord and Lady Heath, no less.

"My dear son!" said Sir William. "What on earth have you been doing with the poor child, and yourself as well; and why?" He looked wryly at the brilliant but torn and dirty garments, the dark stain on their hands and faces, and most particularly at the large hoop earrings on both of them. "Why, you look like Gypsies!"

"Yes," agreed James. "Oh, and by the way, Father, Psammis and his tribe are camped in the south meadow, and I've told them they can stay as long and as often as they like—at least while our family owns Fairlawn."

"Really?" asked his father mildly. "May one ask why?"

"Well, you see—" began James.

Lark came straight to the point. "They saved James's life, for one thing," she said succinctly.

"In that case, there's nothing too good for them," said Lady Trelawney promptly. She and Lark looked at each other with perfect agreement and the dawning of a great understanding. It was clear to both of them that James was quite the most remarkable and altogether wonderful young man on the face of the earth, and this made a very strong bond.

"I want to hear every single thing you've been doing," said Lady Trelawney wistfully. "I suppose, though, you'll want to get washed and changed before you do another thing? Really, James, I *never* thought to see you in quite such a shocking state. And poor Lark . . . Joan, set all our kettles boiling, at once. Are you hungry and tired, too, my dears?"

"As a matter of fact," James said candidly, "we feel fine. We've been traveling quite comfortably with the Gypsies, and we've had plenty of sleep and breakfast; and to tell you the truth, Mother, we're so used to our dirt and rags that I don't really think we'd mind staying this way a little longer. We can't have you perishing of curiosity."

His eyes twinkled at her teasingly, and his father chuckled.

"Shame on you!" said Lady Trelawney with severity. "Are you trying to suggest, my dear James, that your own mother suffers from an excessive amount of curiosity?"

"Yes," said James incorrigibly, and for the next hour

or two they sat comfortably in the big sunny kitchen going over James's various adventures. Joan boiled huge pots of water and listened with her mouth in a round o of amazement, and Gaston hovered in the doorway.

When her curiosity was at least blunted for the time being, Lady Trelawney arose. "Well, I do think there is enough hot water by now even for the two of you," she said. "And I don't mind saying that I shall enjoy the sight of you more when you are clean and presentable. Let me see, now—James, we'll go up and fetch clothing from your room, and then you can bathe in the kitchen here, while Joan and I take Lark upstairs to the tiring room. You would like us to help you, would you not, my dear? And I fear you'll have to wear makeshift clothing for the time being, until we can get something altered or made. Come along."

By this time she had led the way out of the kitchen and along the hall that ran right across the back of the house to a flight of stairs at the far end. Lark could see as they passed through that it led into the main hall and a drawing room, a study, a dining room, and perhaps another drawing room; she wasn't quite sure. But it was a lovely house. Upstairs another hall ran just above the lower one, with windows on one side, bedrooms opening off the other, and family portraits along the walls. Each casement had its window seat, from which she could see the flower garden and the Devon countryside, with just the faintest hint of what might be the sea. Lark very much hoped she was correct in thinking that it might be her home some day.

"You see, your room is just as you left it, James," his mother was saying. "I should think the blue room will do admirably for Lark, and now just as soon as Ned and Giles bring up the hot water—"

At this point she was interrupted by the arrival of a pale and agitated Joan, who ran up the stairs and broke in without so much as a curtsey.

"Oh, Sir William!" she gasped. "T'Roundheads be here! They be at all t'windows all round t'house, sir, and six at t'back door, and two more coming up t'front."

For an instant there was dead silence. Four faces became blank with sudden hard concentration. Three of them were thinking as hard as they could, but Lark (feeling that three better brains than hers were sufficient for thinking) was sending out one of her silent and wordless shouts for help. She didn't specify what kind of help. She felt that God was far more able than she to arrange such matters, and there were already far too many people telling Him exactly what to do. So she just presented Him with the complete problem and a great trust.

It was probably only a few seconds before the other three finished thinking and prepared to act.

"There's no chance at all of getting you out," observed Sir William quietly, glancing out one of the windows to verify Joan's story.

"No," agreed James. "So we'd better stay up here." He looked with satisfaction at the ground-in dirt on himself and Lark, that could not by any chance be taken for a recent disguise. "A good thing we haven't bathed yet," he added, and his parents understood exactly what he had in mind.

"I shall go down to the drawing room and work on my embroidery," announced Lady Trelawney, just as a series of loud knocks thundered through the house. They were the imperious sort of knocks that only a Roundhead was likely to produce.

Sir William raised his eyebrows. "Quite. I shall go to my study. We haven't seen you of course, son. Joan, go down to the kitchen and get ready to use all that hot water for whatever you do with hot water. Pretend it's yesterday, and tell them whatever they may ask."

Joan fled. The knocking came again. Sir William chuckled. "Gaston will take his own good time about answering it," he observed. "He doesn't care for people who knock that way. Bless you, son." He pressed his hand on James's shoulder, straightened his own shoulders a trifle, and walked down the stairs with every appearance of leisurely calm.

James swallowed in pride for them, then grabbed Lark's hand and tiptoed into his parents' bedroom just as the measured tread of Gaston moved with disapproving dignity toward the front door.

19
The Intruders

Lady Trelawney sat at her embroidery frame, her back to the door. "Whoever it was, Gaston," she said as she heard his quiet feet behind her, "I am quite sure we don't know them. *None* of our friends would think of knocking in that impolite fashion."

"It's two—uh—persons from the Parliament army," announced Gaston with clear distaste. "They wish to see Sir William, m'Lady."

Lady Trelawney turned and surveyed the Major and foot trooper who stood there. "Really?" she said without much interest. "I can't think why. In any event, he's in his study, and would dislike it very much if anyone were to disturb him there. Perhaps you may speak to him another time."

The trooper looked intimidated at this, but the officer

bristled. "Army business," he snapped. "Do not try to delay me, madam. Send for Sir William at once. I don't care in the least whether he likes it or not."

"That's because you are not married to him," pointed out Lady Trelawney reasonably. "I am, and I *do* care. Perhaps you will tell me your business."

Gaston had momentary difficulty controlling his expression, but neither of the soldiers noticed it. The major, who was liking Lady Trelawney less and less by the minute, stiffened. "Very well, I *shall* tell you," he replied, a gleam of spite in his eyes. "If you insist, madam. But you had best prepare yourself for a shock, and don't say I didn't try to spare you. The fact is, madam, I've a warrant here for the arrest of your son, James Trelawney."

He looked maliciously at Lady Trelawney, who confused him by relaxing visibly. "Oh, is *that* all!" she said in evident relief. "It's all right then, Gaston; we shan't have to disturb Sir William at all. I was afraid," she explained, turning back to the major, "that you had come to put us out of our house or something, and I assure you, my husband would have been *most* seriously annoyed."

"But he doesn't mind having his son arrested?" the major managed to demand sarcastically. He had just about decided that the lady's wits were addled.

"Oh, that!" She fluttered her hand at him. "You see, that's simply a silly mistake. I'm sure it wasn't your fault; probably a general or someone. I've noticed that very often the most important men are the most muddle-headed, don't you think? At any rate, I can't possibly think why anyone should want to arrest my Jamikins. For one thing he's only a boy, and for another he isn't even here. He's way off in

Kent, visiting his grandmama, and has been all summer. Why do they say they want to arrest him, by the way?"

The major was having some difficulty keeping his mind on the subject. "For treason, madam," he said stiffly. "Aiding and abetting one Charles Stewart."

"Oh, now, isn't that silly?" Lady Trelawney laughed. "They have the wrong person altogether, of course. You had better go back and tell them—"

"Sorry, ma'am," interrupted the major, confused but deeply suspicious. "I have my orders, and if you don't produce your son at once, I must search the house. As you see, he can't possibly get away with my men surrounding the house, so there's no point in wasting my time any longer."

Lady Trelawney frowned at him. "You know," she decided, "I don't believe I care at all for your manners. Search the house, indeed! Why, you weren't even *invited* here. And as for wasting time, it's quite the other way round. It is *you* who are interrupting *me*, and if you had any idea how much there is to do—"

At this point there was the sound of a door opening in the hall behind Gaston, and a muffled bellow which indicated that Sir William had been listening carefully and was determined to live up to the reputation his wife had given him.

"What in thunderation—Gaston! Katherine! Am I never to be allowed a moment of peace? What in blazes is all that noise?"

"You see?" Lady Trelawney looked reproachfully at the major and turned to call past Gaston in soothing tones. "Don't bother, dear; it's quite all right. Merely a silly muddle about wanting to arrest little Jamie for treason, but I'm explaining to the man that it's all a mistake."

"It is *not* a mistake!" interrupted the major hastily and loudly. He felt that he would much prefer even an infuriated Sir William to his idiotic wife. "I have a warrant, and I warn you that I shall be obliged to search your house if you don't producc James Trelawney."

Sir William suddenly appeared in the doorway, looking so choleric that the major almost changed his mind, and even the pokerfaced Gaston looked surprised. "What? What? Stuff and nonsense! Never heard such lunacy!" He scowled at the major, who backed up one step, recovered, and waved his warrant in Sir William's face. Sir William grabbed it, read it, appeared about to choke, and shoved it aside.

"Lunacy!" he repeated. "Boy's not even here. Hasn't been for months. Sent him away out of trouble. Gross inefficiency!" He glared at the officer, who glared back, determined not to give in an inch.

"You see, you've annoyed him!" cried Lady Trelawney accusingly. "William, dear, why not just let them go on and search, so they can go away again? Although I do think it very bad manners to go poking around in people's private homes, and I shall be most offended if you damage anything or let your soldiers go into my wardrobe. What do you think, William?"

Sir William grunted disagreeably. "Oh, very well; hurry and get it over. I trust the two of you are capable of it without turning your whole army loose in my house? And mind, I shall be behind you every minute, so you need not try to filch anything."

The major flushed hotly, controlled himself, and followed a stiffly disapproving Gaston through the lower part of the house. In any other Royalist house, he would have left a swath of destruction behind. It was a matter of principle among many Parliament soldiers to smash breakables, slash portraits and hangings, and generally destroy as much as possible. Unfortunately, this pleasure was denied the major in this particular house, for he had been ordered not to damage anything. It seemed that one Nathaniel Beveys, a friend of General Cromwell himself, had expressed a wish for this estate once things were settled down a little, and he wanted it in good condition. The major fumed silently, but didn't dare put his sword through so much as a single chair.

They paused in the kitchen. The major questioned the blank-faced Joan while his trooper looked under tables and in tubs and up the fireplace. Joan was of no help at all. She said the young master was away, and she minded it were in late spring he left, about cherry blooming time, or just after, and she couldn't rightly mind where he'd went, but he'd forgot his new blue coat, and a pity that was, too.

Feeling more and more out of temper, the major continued to follow Gaston along the hall, up the stairs, and, with a glance out the windows to make sure his men were still at their posts, he began on the upstairs rooms. He was beginning to have a sour suspicion that this trip was not going to be at all successful, but he certainly was not going to give up without covering every inch of ground, even to the point of searching Lady Trelawney's wardrobe. Yes, definitely he would do that: it would infuriate her.

But he didn't get quite that far, after all. It was from

under the massive four-poster bed in the large bedroom that his trooper flushed the quarry. There was a muffled squeak, a scuffling sound, and then a yelp from the soldier, who backed out nursing a bit finger.

"Mercy!" said Lady Trelawney, looking deeply interested.

"Come out this instant!" the major called under the bed. "Do you hear? If you don't, I shall shoot."

"I should consider that excessively ill-mannered," declared Lady Trelawney decidedly.

Nobody paid any attention to her. There was a shuffling sound from beneath the bed. After a moment, on the far side, two apparitions arose, slowly, side by side.

They really looked most startling against the clean and austere richness of the bedroom. Their hair was tangled wildly, the dirt on their skins and clothing showed up admirably, and they wore expressions of guilty cheekiness borrowed directly from Bracken. Moreover, Lark was wearing one of Lady Trelawney's lace collars over her own gaudy beads and trying to hide a handful of satin ribbands; while James clutched a pair of silver shoe buckles.

There was quite a long silence.

"My best shoe buckles!" said Sir William at last in a strangled voice.

James looked sheepish, but only slightly.

"I am extremely tired," Lady Trelawney announced in plaintive tones, "of having people come into my home without being invited. I do wish you would *all* go away—and leave our property behind when you go. What *are* you naughty children doing here, anyway?" she added quite unnecessarily.

Lark smiled at her shamelessly. "Read your palm, Lady?" she suggested in Willow's best manner and accent. "I will tell you a very good fortune."

"How can you do that?" demanded Lady Trelawney, momentarily sidetracked. "If you read the lines on my palm, I mean, and the future is already set, how can you know before you look whether it will be good or simply dreadful?"

"Oh, I can tell—" began Lark, but Sir William began to rumble ominously, and his wife hastily waved her hands at the Gypsies.

"Never mind that now," she said. "You are very naughty, and we are *most* displeased." She frowned at them. "When we gave your people permission to camp in our meadow, we never for one *minute* intended that you should come sneaking into our house and steal our things. You ought to be ashamed of yourselves."

James and Lark contrived to look nothing of the sort; only slightly inconvenienced at having been caught.

Lady Trelawney blinked at them and turned to her husband. "William, do you think they *entirely* understand about Good and Evil?"

"I should consider it highly doubtful," replied Sir William, looking grim. He was clearly working up to a simply deafening explosion. One could almost begin to see the black smoke escaping from his nose and mouth.

No one had been paying the slightest attention to the Roundheads for several minutes now, and it began to occur to the major that the situation was rapidly escaping from his hands—if indeed it had ever been there at all.

He cleared his throat. It was intended to be a masterful sound, but it somehow came out a trifle tentative. He tried again with better results. Everyone turned and looked at him, and he began to wish that he felt more sure of his ground, especially with Sir William glowering like that from beneath what could only be described as beetled brows.

"Are you James Trelawney?" he demanded of James, and immediately felt extremely foolish. Even his trooper looked at him as if he had lost his wits. James and Lark regarded him with pitying curiosity, and then turned their attention back to Sir William, who was now turning a most unwholesome shade of red.

"Oh, dear!" Lady Trelawney looked at the major impatiently. "Major, do please *try* not to be so silly! Can't you see how vexed he's getting? William, my love, don't you think we should send these very dirty young persons back to their camp? And I think Hal should go along to see that they go straight there, and also to tell the Gypsies that if this sort of thing happens again, we shall be very seriously displeased."

"No!" growled Sir William. "Not Hal. I'll escort them back myself." He looked pleased with the prospect. "Come along!"

The major asserted himself. "I'm going to finish searching!" he declared loudly.

Sir William turned and looked at him. He smiled. The major didn't at all like the smile.

"Yes, by heaven, you are!" agreed Sir William softly. "You are going to search every inch of this house, my good fellow, and I shall personally make sure you do a good job of it. Gaston, kindly stay here with these young rogues until I am ready to take them back to their camp. Major, be kind enough to come with me. We are about to search,

Major." And he led the way out of the room, with the soldiers behind him and Lady Trelawney bringing up the rear, calling to him to please remember his heart.

The instant the door was safely shut, with the impassive Gaston standing guard just outside, Lark sank on her knees and buried her face in the bedclothes to muffle her giggles. "Oh, James!" she whispered as he dropped down beside her, "Your parents are wonderful! I adore them both, and your mother was so funny I could scarcely keep from laughing!"

James grinned, quite at ease now that his father had things well in hand. "Actually," he murmured, "Mother's a born comic, so I've no doubt it was quite easy for her. But you know Father is the mildest-tempered man in the world." He shook his head in admiration of his father's dramatic ability. "I'd like to invite you to sit in a comfortable chair, Lark, but . . ." He looked at the fine tapestried padding on his mother's favorite chair sadly, and then at Lark's garments.

"Another time." Lark cocked her head at James and settled herself comfortably on a plain wooden chair beside the wardrobe chest. "I wonder how that poor Roundhead is getting along."

The poor Roundhead was getting along very miserably indeed. He was, as promised, being given a very thorough search. Sir William stood over him and saw to it that every chest, box, drawer, window seat, and corner in every room was gone into.

"Behind the hangings, there," ordered Sir William. "You forgot to look under that cushion. Joan, empty that sewing box for the major."

It was not at all the sort of search the major had visualized. He was not used to such high-handed enthusiasm from people whose homes were being searched. But there was not a thing he could do about it except fume silently. He finished with a sense of great relief, left two of his soldiers there to keep an eye on things, and led the rest of them back to headquarters feeling sullen and altogether frustrated.

20
The Way to France

A short time later Sir William Trelawney and his wife marched with purpose and majesty from their front door, followed by Gaston herding two disreputable Gypsies in front of him. The two Parliament soldiers on guard looked at the procession and each other doubtfully; then one of them followed discreetly behind while the other kept watch over the house.

The procession, still with immense dignity—or at least the first portion of it—strode straight to the south meadow where the Gypsies were camped. There Sir William exchanged a few words with Psammis and Sheba which the trailing Roundhead could not hear, but which looked to him like an approaching storm.

After that, Psammis, Sheba, and the procession vanished into the yellow wagon, leaving the Roundhead nothing to look at but Neco sitting carelessly on the steps and a sudden swarm of Gypsy children who were making as much noise as possible. Led by a demon of a small boy, they raced and shrieked around the yellow wagon so that only now and then could the Roundhead hear roars of rage from inside. But he did not altogether like the looks that the Gypsies were giving him, so he withdrew to the edge of the meadow. After all, he pointed out to himself, an argument between an ungodly Royalist and an even more ungodly Gypsy was hardly important to General Cromwell.

Lark sat on the floor inside the wagon next to James, leaving what seats there were to his parents. She had been considerably upset to hear that the Roundheads really meant to arrest and hang James if they could only lay their hands on him. She was glad that the grownups had enough sense not to fuss about unimportant details such as class barriers or dirt, but got straight to the heart of the matter, which was to get James safely out of England as quickly as possible.

"I'm afraid we must call on your further kindness," said Sir William to Psammis. "It seems clear that they must remain Gypsies for a while longer."

Psammis did not look overjoyed at this, for even though he understood that Sir William's gratitude would be great and tangible and probably of gold, there was more danger to the tribe now, with a warrant out for James. But Sheba gave him no time to object.

"Yes!" she said firmly, speaking to Lady Trelawney in particular. "For if you first gave life to your son, I gave it to him again, and share motherhood with you. Moreover," she added, "I foresee that you will be with him again soon, but it will be many years for me, so it is fair that I keep him now."

"Well, if it comes to that," James murmured into Lark's ear, "you saved my life too, you know; probably twice."

"I am *not* going to think of myself as your mother!" retorted Lark with great firmness, and James choked slightly.

Lady Trelawney was nodding sadly to Sheba. "Yes," she said. "You can help him now, and we cannot. I suppose we dare not even see him again before he leaves, for there is certain to be some crop-headed, psalm-chanting trooper at our heels from now on."

"And very unsettling you'll make it for them, too, my dear," added her husband cheerfully. "However, I fear we shan't be able to help James get transportation to France now, without endangering all of you and anyone else we contacted. . . ." He sat for a moment, frowning at nothing, while he concentrated.

"Never mind, Father; I can do that better than you, anyway," announced James. "I know nearly every Royalist in Devon, I dare say. And I'm already on the track of a man who comes over here quite often just to find people like me to spirit away from under Roundhead noses. And I fancy we could risk letting Bracken drop by the house quite often, Mother, to pass on any news and let you know when and where we've gone."

"We?" echoed Lady Trelawney, looking at Lark. "James, I really don't think you should try to take Lark! Why, you've already dragged that poor, delicately nurtured child (James hooted at this description, and Lark pinched him) over half of England, and now you're proposing to take her into a foreign country, not particularly civilized in some ways, I gather, just on the chance that her parents might be there somewhere. It's bad enough for *you* to go off that way, my dear; I really think it would be much better to leave Lark with us until we can join you."

"Join me?" echoed James, holding Lark's hand possessively, but momentarily distracted.

"Certainly," said his father. "You don't think we'd let you go off into indefinite exile alone, do you? We'll be along as soon as we can arrange our affairs here."

"But the house! Fairlawn!" protested James.

"That's all arranged," Sir William answered, looking faintly smug. "Your mother's cousin Nathaniel Beveys put in his request for it to Cromwell himself, and it's been granted him to take over at his pleasure. Nathaniel's a fine man, even though I consider him to have taken his loyalty to the wrong side, and he's very fond of your mother. All we need do is let him know we're leaving, and he'll take care of it for us until such a time as we may be able to return."

"Oh," said James in great relief, and turned his attention back to the problem of Lark. "I can't leave her behind," he discovered with satisfaction. "It would be too dangerous. People might ask questions, or her uncle might find her."

"Anyhow," added Lark, looking conceited, "he needs me. He's safer when I'm around."

Lady Trelawney surrendered without another word. Then there were a few details like money and how to exchange messages to settle, and after that it was high time for half the procession to go back.

Psammis and Sir William suddenly remembered to shout and roar at each other again, but this time on a friendlier note, to indicate to the audience that a truce was being reached. Lady Trelawney, keeping her feelings admirably under control, kissed James and Lark lightly.

"God bless you both and keep you safe, my dears," she said. And the conference emerged from the yellow wagon with an air of much dignity and rather cautious good will.

For the next two days, the Gypsies scattered around the countryside, the men with their tinkering tools, the girls and women to tell fortunes. James and Lark also roamed around, but with a more direct purpose. It was not to be expected that the Gypsies would learn anything helpful except by accident, since the Romany and the Gorgio were not in the habit of confiding in each other on matters of life and death.

But James very quickly picked up a hint that young gentlemen anxious to leave the country in a hurry for their health might do well to wander around the Dart River and the streams that fed into it. He didn't need a second hint.

By the afternoon of the second day he and Lark were hot on the trail of the gentleman with the boat, and were walking into a small village consisting mainly of a few thatched cottages, a smithy, and an inn situated on the banks of a wide stream. The inn served without doubt as local meeting place, clubhouse, and tavern, and there was a walled garden with benches between the inn and the banks of the stream.

Lark eyed the inn with some apprehension, feeling that so far their luck in such places had not been altogether good. James hesitated for the more practical reason that Gypsies could hardly walk right in and ask for "a gentleman who was helping Royalists escape"—especially since he didn't happen to know any Royalists in this particular village. So he and Lark wandered around a little, peered into the blacksmith's shop, and presently paused to glance through the open gate into the inn yard.

Instantly they heard a most familiar voice.

"I can tell that you are a most clever and good woman, and so I shall tell you a very good fortune for only a small piece of silver."

"Willow!" whispered Lark, standing on tiptoe to see over the shrubbery and James. But all she could make out was a swinging gold earring amid dark hair, and beyond it the barest glimpse of what seemed to be an elderly farm woman.

"Shhh," said James, who could see a bit more, and wanted to hear more, too. Willow's chosen victim had a trusting and gullible expression that at once aroused his sense of chivalry, and he did not intend just to stand there and let her be cheated.

"Eh," said the victim. "Tis fine and good of ee, m'dear, but what wid an old woman th' loikes of oi do wi' silver?"

"Surely you have one piece?" Willow wheedled. "Silver brings much better luck than copper, and I can tell a much better for—" There was a smart slapping sound, and she interrupted her own speech with a small yelp of pain and surprise.

"Eh, m'dear," came the woman's voice as Willow nursed a stinging wrist. "Oi never telled ee to look in oi's purse ee'self, now, did I?" Her voice was placid and slow, but there was a hidden note of tart humor that caused Lark to burrow her way past James in order to get a good look at its owner.

"Grandmother!" she squealed, and under the dumbfounded noses of James and Willow, she hurled herself across the courtyard and into the farm woman's arms.

The farm woman, after one instant of blank amazement, bore up very well. A pair of tip-tilted green eyes sparkled, and she held Lark at arm's length to survey her. "I always did say you took after me," she remarked with satisfaction. "Knew you'd be too much for Jeremiah. Well? Did you run away, or did he give up and turn you out?"

Lark giggled. James stood where he was and went on staring. Could it be . . . Was it possible that the redoubtable grandmother . . . the highborn lady who spoke her mind to kings . . . was now wandering Devon disguised as a poor country woman? . . . The more James looked at that vital face, the more he thought that this unlikely notion was, after all, highly probable. He also thought he could now guess from whom Lark had gotten certain traits of character.

"What are you doing here, Grandmother?" Lark was now demanding. "I knew you'd be doing something exciting! Is Grandfather here, too? Oh, I know! Is he the gentleman who comes around to save Royalists from the Roundheads and whisk them off to France? He is, isn't he? And you . . ." She paused, and her mind flew back to the Blue Dolphin and certain other parts of her journey with James. "You're very useful, aren't you, Grandmother?" she chortled. "Who would suspect Grandfather when he has his dear sweet wife along?"

Lark was very nearly beside herself with excitement. Lady Valerie held her peace and waited for the spate of words to subside.

"Are you going to save us? You must, you know, because James and I do need saving, especially James. . . . Oh!" She whirled, her face suddenly puckered with remorse, to drag James forward. "Oh, I *am* sorry! This is James Trelawney, Grandmother, and we've been saving each other from Roundheads and things, and he's taken *very* good care of me. And you mustn't blame him for my running away," she added, correctly interpreting a severe flash in Lady Valerie's eyes. "He hadn't anything to do with it, and he couldn't take me back, because I wouldn't tell him where. And you can't scold *me* for running away, either," she went on with an engaging but impudent grin. "Just think how many times you've told me the story about how you and Grandfather *both* ran away when you were young, and met at the players', and played Romeo and Juliet, and fell in love; and if you did, why shouldn't I?"

"Which?" demanded her grandmother meaningfully. "Run away, or play Juliet, or fall in love?"

Lark turned pink and declined to answer, but James, mercifully, did not notice. "I know who you are, Ma'am," he said, bowing deeply. "I've been wishing to meet you. You're the lady who tells kings and queens to their faces that they are idiots."

Lady Valerie smiled, greatly pleased. "Only when they deserve it," she amended. "However, I must admit that this has been very frequently since our Queen Bess died. Not that I should have told *her* such a thing even if she had deserved it," she admitted.

James, looking at her, didn't believe this for a moment, and said so. But Lady Valerie shook her head.

"You never saw her," she said. "She kept three steps ahead of the rest of the world, Queen Elizabeth did."

At that point a shabby, white-haired old man came out of the inn and paused in the courtyard to stare for a moment. Then he suddenly ceased to resemble a poor countryman, by the simple process of straightening up, throwing back his thick hair like a lion tossing its mane, and giving a delighted roar.

"Lark, you young scamp! What in blazes are you doing here and in that outfit when you're supposed to be in durance vile at the hands of Jeremiah? Where did you find her, Val?"

He looked a little like King Lear, and sounded like Hamlet, so that James could very easily see him running away to adventure with the players as a boy, and playing roles well, too. Neither he nor his wife, in fact, seemed to have given up play-acting at all.

Willow interrupted at this point, rather acidly. "I do not know what is happening," she remarked, "but I think that if anyone sees an old Gorgio man hugging a Gypsy girl they will be very much astounded, and will want to know more. I would also be very glad if someone explains to me all the nonsense you have been talking, and how people like you could be talking to kings and queens."

Lark and her grandfather hastily separated, and Lady Valerie looked at Willow with a twinkle. "You're quite right, and I think we had best start being practical at once," she said. "Is this young lady a friend of yours, Lark? Well, then, you shall have your bit of silver, though you don't really deserve it, you know. A clumsier attempt at picking a purse I have seldom seen."

Willow, who prided herself on her light fingers, gave an outraged gasp, snatched at the coin Lady Valerie held out to her, and stalked away in great mortification. James grinned after her retreating back as it whisked out of the gate, stared thoughtfully for just an instant, and turned back to be properly introduced to Sir Nicholas Raven. Then he got down to business.

"If you *are* the gentleman with the boat whom we've been hunting, sir, do you suppose we could leave quite soon? Things," he added with modest understatement, "have been getting a bit warm lately."

"By all means," agreed Sir Nicholas at once, "Have you any preparations to make? Anyone to notify? Your parents?"

James's glance flickered briefly in the direction of the gate. "Oh, I'm sure Willow will tell Psammis and Sheba, and they'll tell Mother and Father," he said lightly. "Willow is a *very* clever girl. Besides, she knows Father will see that she gets a gold piece—the very minute he hears we're safe in France, that is," he added with sudden prudence.

Sir Nicholas nodded and also eyed the open gate. There was a tiny speck of green in the crack which did not seem quite to match any of the foliage. "Splendid," he said affably. "I hope she's also clever enough to realize that she can earn more gold by faithfully carrying any message for you?"

"She is," broke in Lark firmly. "You see, her mother has rather adopted James because of saving his life, so you see they can absolutely be trusted to the death to keep faith, and help."

Sir Nicholas nodded. "In that case, I hope Willow stays right where she is, for I have a bit of business to discuss with her and the innkeeper. I'll settle our reckoning at the same time, Val, so we can leave at once."

He strode out of the courtyard looking as commanding and purposeful as Othello, leaving James with his mouth open, ready to explain about leaving a message so that his parents could find him when they came to France. Sir Nicholas having already taken himself out of hearing, James explained this to Lady Valerie instead. She merely nodded.

"Yes, Nick will have guessed that," she said briskly. "It's one of the things he's arranging."

"But—" began James. "How? Where?"

"You'll stay with Lark's family and us, of course," Lady Valerie told him masterfully. "We've a very nice chateau near the coast with plenty of room. When your parents are ready, we'll fetch them ourselves, Nick and I. We come over quite regularly." She turned to include Lark in her smile. It was clear that she was enjoying herself very much, and James wondered briefly how she and his mother would get on. Then he pulled himself back to the present hastily, because Lady Valerie was giving directions.

"We've a dory hidden upstream, and our boat is waiting for us down in the river estuary. But it won't do to set village tongues wagging by being seen just now with you disreputable children. After all, Nick and I have our respectable roles to maintain. You two will have to slip out back of the inn, here, and walk downstream until you reach a sharp bend about half a mile on, with a clump of willows right at the point. We'll be along presently in the dory and pick you up there."

She ushered them right out of a small back gate as

she spoke, and they found themselves, a trifle breathless, looking across a short stretch of green meadow to the darker green line where the stream flowed. James took a deep breath, cocked his head, and regarded Lark with a grin that she found completely mystifying.

"Don't you like Grandmother and Grandfather?" she asked.

"Oh, very much indeed!" he told her truthfully. "Life couldn't possibly be dull with them around, could it?" But his grin broadened. He was thinking that, after all, perhaps Lark wasn't quite as strong-willed and managing a person as he had thought her. Compared to her grandmother, in fact, she was a most tractable and compliant small person, and James had no doubt at all that they would get on extremely well together.

"Come on," he said, holding out his hand. And although she teased all the way to the clump of willows, he did not tell her what he had been grinning about.

21
The Equinox

It was almost an anticlimax. They sailed down the stream and the river, found the *Sea Raven,* and sailed out of the estuary without so much as a scare or a false alarm. Lark felt rather cheated. Not that she wanted any more *real* trouble for a while yet, but one more dramatic episode might have been fun before settling down to a life of dull safety in France. But it didn't look for a while as if anything of the sort was going to happen, even though they sailed along the south coast of England close enough to keep a fairly sharp eye on the shore.

"Far enough out to be safe," Sir Nicholas told James, "but near enough for practical purposes. You see, the fishermen along here know my boat. Royalist ones, anyway. They'll signal if they should happen to have a message or a passenger for me."

It was near the Isle of Wight that the signal came.

"An urgent one," said Grandfather, his lean old face sparkling with interest. "I presume there's some poor Royalist in there just a nip and two inches ahead of the Roundheads. We'll lay offshore until dark, and then take the small boat in and see if we can get him off."

"May I go?" demanded Lark and James at once.

"Certainly not," said Sir Nicholas. "I'll take two of my own crew. No one in the world can handle boats and currents better." Then he paused, looked thoughtful, and changed his mind. "On second thought, I'll take James if he'd like to go."

Lark stuck out her lip in annoyance as her grandfather turned to one of his crew. It really was too bad being left behind while James went off adventuring without her! Unfair!

"What's the date?" demanded Grandfather suddenly turning from his conference. "I thought so! September twenty-first, the exact top of the autumn equinox. *And* a full moon tonight as well. We'll have the highest tide tonight that's been seen in some years, I fancy!"

James remembered some of his history. "Wasn't it the equinox high tides and storms that wrecked Julius Caesar's fleet two years in a row when he was trying to invade Britain?" he asked.

Sir Nicholas nodded, and Helier, a French mariner who had been first mate of the *Sea Raven* ever since it was built, spoke up in his oddly French-flavored English.

"The storm, she comes, too, her." He glanced westward at the gray ocean, heaving a little with long swells. "She sits and waits. Presently, after midnight I think, she begins to arrive herself. I think perhaps she will be one like that of 1647, one big killer, that. We should set sail before dawn if we do not wish to smash ourselves in small pieces on the rocks."

Sir Nicholas nodded. "If anything should delay us," he told his wife, "don't wait too long. I'll leave Helier on board, and you'll sail when he says, whether we're back or not."

Lark caught her breath at this, and was astonished that her grandmother's face was perfectly serene.

"Very well, Nick. In that case, I'd come back for you, of course, as soon as possible."

And Grandfather nodded again, matter-of-factly.

Lark fumed and puzzled inwardly while they had a bite of supper and waited for dark. It was dangerous! Grandfather and James might not get back in time, might be caught, might have to be abandoned to the mercies of Cromwell's men! Didn't Grandmother even *care?* Why didn't she say anything? She might have been seeing them off on a pheasant hunt!

But when Lark started to object, she found her grandmother's green eyes on her, and felt a warning tap. Grandmother wasn't a person to be defied casually, so Lark held her tongue and clenched her teeth. She kept silent while James and Grandfather disappeared—probably forever—over the rail in the white light of the full moon.

Very near tears, Lark glanced up at her grandmother a little resentfully, envying her that unshakeable calm. Then she nearly yelped aloud for Grandmother was gripping her hand so fiercely that Lark was sure every finger must be squashed to a pulp! Astonished, she realized that Grandmother was not in the least tranquil, but merely a remarkable actress.

Lark, who had rather prided herself for her own acting

ability, regarded her cheerful face with awe, and almost forgot her distress in wonder and admiration.

The air was very calm, but the sea was a little agitated now. Large swells, higher now, indicated the storm still to the west; and a great confusion of the smaller waves told a story to sea-wise eyes of equinox, tides, and currents. Lark, fascinated by the menace of that sea, felt no desire to go down to the cabin and wait. She stared down at the silvery dark lapping against the yacht, and felt Grandmother's stillness beside her.

"So you've been growing up, have you?" murmured Lady Valerie. "I see you've even followed the family tradition of selecting your own man and sharing a few adventures with him."

"Yes, but *he* hasn't got around to selecting *me* yet." grumbled Lark. "And now he's off having adventures without me."

"That's your next step in growing up," remarked Grandmother with a chuckle that was not unsympathetic. "Learn when to let your man go off into danger, and do not cry, nor try to hold him back, nor ask to go with him."

Lark disliked this idea very much, and said so. She hadn't liked it when she first started chewing on it way back in Shrewsbury, and she didn't like it any better now, and she had once thought that she would *never* be able to swallow it. But if even Grandmother said it was necessary . . . Lark tightened her lips in one last surge of rebellion. Then she melted in sudden love for James, and a saintly feeling that she would suffer anything at all to make him happy.

Lark being human, the saintliness vanished almost at once, and she found herself explaining her complicated feelings to her grandmother, who said that she understood and sympathized perfectly. "Unfortunately," she said, "one has to give a little sometimes."

Lark looked at her reproachfully in the gloom of the night sky. Grandmother? Compromise? Lady Valerie smiled ruefully, seeming to read her mind.

"It isn't that I don't believe in meeting life head-on," she explained, "because I do. And I've found that a little determination can often do wonders to rearrange things in a very satisfactory way. But," she added regretfully, "not always. You have to learn where to compromise, and it's love that will teach you best."

Lark conceded the point because her heart knew it to be true. Still, even the most dangerous and disagreeable adventure was much better than being left behind. She knew. She had tried both. And danger did add a distinct zest to life. It was a challenge to one's cleverness and courage, she explained earnestly, and things promised to be so dull when they reached the safety of France.

"I shouldn't worry about that *yet*," warned her grandmother. "I can see you've become addicted to adventure, poppet, and I can quite sympathize with you. But that doesn't alter what I said in the least. If you love your husband, be able to let him go sometimes."

If men loved *us*, they ought to realize how awful it is to be left behind!" retorted Lark. "After all, if we're the weaker sex and need to be cherished and cared for, why can't we just explain that it's really *much* harder—"

"Fiddlesticks!" interrupted Lady Valerie briskly. "Most men think that, poor dears, and even a good many women, I dare say. But I know better, and I think you do, too.

Women, my dear Lark, are a great deal stronger in some ways than men."

Lark looked surprised at this, and her grandmother laughed.

"Oh, not in size or weight or muscle, of course. But we can endure better—both physical pain and things like fear and uncertainty and worry. And since God has given us this special sort of strength, presumably He expects us to use it."

Lark considered this for a moment, in high disapproval. It really seemed most unfair of God . . . and just when she was beginning to get on with Him so well, too. She sighed impatiently. Then she remembered that she had already made quite a start in training James. With any luck, he was already so addicted to having Lark along on adventures that she would be able to share them more often than not, just as Grandmother did, now that she came to think of it. Feeling considerably more cheerful, she put her mind once more on the matter of what might be happening on shore.

Midnight drew near. The sea was growing more restless. Waves were both higher and choppier, and odd, cold, menacing little gusts of wind began to blow from the west. Helier faced into it, frowning and sniffing, and a perfectly awful fear clutched more and more firmly at Lark. Grandfather and James had almost certainly been captured by the Roundheads! Perhaps they had been shot as well! It was all she could do not to burst into sobs, but she didn't, because Grandmother would be very much ashamed of her if she did, and Grandmother herself must be feeling sick with worry.

So Lark managed somehow to keep her face in the shadow and her voice steady as midnight came and passed. Her conversation with God became more and more urgent. Then there was a bumping sound at the side of the boat, and a cheerful hail announced that everything had gone beautifully.

Lark sat down suddenly on the deck, dizzy with relief. For a moment she wanted to burst into wild tears. Then she wanted to explode into a violent temper tantrum. How could they be so *nonchalant*? Selfish beasts! Didn't they—

Lark heard James's voice as he climbed over the rail just behind the rescued Cavaliers, and she decided against the tantrum, or even the tears. For one thing, it was enough that he was safe, and for another, there was a certain note in his voice that caused her to forget about her grievance.

She moved forward quickly, picking out James in the white moonlight. He was staring at the tallest refugee with a look of suppressed excitement. Lark stared, too. He was an exceedingly tall young man, with a long, swarthy, knobbly face, and dark cropped hair.

"Mercy!" said Lark uncertainly. Was it possible?

It was. James's manner showed it, and Grandmother recognized him at once, even before Grandfather climbed briskly over the rail and told them to pay their respects to His Majesty King Charles II.

"Mercy!" said Lark again, thinking in confusion that he had not really changed, except to grow even larger, since he used to visit her brother and sister in Oxford. And oh, dear! How awful if no one had seen the signal from shore and stopped to rescue him!

"I think Charles will forgive us if we postpone our respects," suggested Grandmother practically. "Helier says we should get under way at once if we want to reach Ravenhurst in one piece, and I rather think Charles could use a bite to eat and a glass of wine, and possibly even a bit of sleep."

"Madam, I'd give a kingdom for them if I had a kingdom to give," said Charles with wry humor.

22
Charles

By daylight the little boat was running under a full gale, with Helier cheerfully predicting worse to come. The king's loyal companion, Lord Wilmot, failed to appear for breakfast, the storm not agreeing with him at all. But Lark and James both found it extremely stimulating and exactly to their taste, and King Charles seemed to have a very seagoing nature too.

All three of them wanted to know if they could help handle the boat, but the crew merely smiled at them with kindly contempt for landlubbers, and indicated that they would be of most use safely inside. Even Grandfather, looking rather like Prospero from *The Tempest* this morning, was not allowed to do much more than stand on deck.

"Helier will shoo him back in presently," said Grandmother.

It was too rough for a fire in the galley, so they were

having a cold breakfast in the small and crowded cabin "drawing room," feeling altogether satisfied with themselves, while Charles told of his hair-raising escapes. He had hidden in an oak tree while Roundheads searching for him walked directly beneath. He had been chased and almost caught at the Welsh border. He had ridden to Bristol as a groom behind the most remarkable lady named Jane Lane. He had, like James and Lark, stayed at Heale House; and what with one thing and another he had managed to get nearly to Southampton without ever a chance to cross the Channel.

"Until now," he added. "I'm extremely grateful. Also, I might add, most impressed with your rescue operations . . . complete with pretty girls!" And he smiled warmly at Lark, who blushed and smiled back.

James frowned. It was well known that Charles was excessively fond of pretty girls, who, in turn, usually found him altogether fascinating.

"I'm not sure you really deserved rescuing at all," remarked Lady Valerie briskly. "You *have* been making a pretty fool of yourself this last year or so, haven't you?"

Charles, not really used to this sort of plain speaking except from the Scots, turned in considerable astonishment and stared at Lady Valerie, who returned his gaze calmly. Then he began to grin.

"It's been a long time, but I remember you very well!" he said. "You used to drop in now and then to say that sort of thing to Father."

"And his father before him," agreed Lady Valerie equably. "And now you. I dare say idiocy must run in the family."

Charles shouted with laughter and then sobered. "Possibly you're right," he mused. "Father used to be upset after your visits, and Mam was always furious—but perhaps if Father had listened to you, he might be alive today."

"Don't try to rearrange the past," advised Lady Valerie gently. "It's not too late for *you* to begin acting intelligently, though. Who knows, if you'll take my advice you might even sit on that throne of yours some day, and not by conquest, either. . . . Lark, pour His Majesty some more ale, poppet."

"Lark?" Charles looked at her again, to James's increasing disapproval. "Of course! Cecily's baby sister! How *very* pretty you've grown, sweet Lark!"

At that moment James could cheerfully have pitched his King overboard. Sweet Lark, indeed! That was *his* name for her! He had, he decided, put up with quite enough.

"Excuse me!" he said, standing up suddenly. "There's something very urgent that I have to tell Lark. This minute."

He seized her by the arm in a grip that would ordinarily have caused her to box his ears. Instead, she gave him a melting smile and permitted herself to be marched to the door like a perfect lamb.

James had every intention of hurling the door open and sweeping Lark across the deck to the bow, where he could propose in the teeth of the howling storm, with spray flying before them. This was less romantic than moonlight and balconies, but James was really more in the mood for a dramatic setting, anyway. He pushed furiously at the door.

It opened a full two inches, admitted a blast of wind and drenching spray, and slammed shut again.

James and Lark regarded it with amazement. They had never been in a storm at sea before, and had quite underestimated the violence of this one. As if to make sure that they appreciated it now, the boat gave a particularly boisterous heave, jerk, and roll, which caused them to clutch each other and stagger against the bulkhead.

James perceived at once that the bow would never do for intimate conversation—nor, for that matter would anywhere else on deck. On the other hand, he was not going to retreat now, especially with Lady Valerie and the king sitting there watching him with interest. There was only one thing to do.

James abandoned his dramatic setting along with the romantic one, turned on his heel, and marched himself and Lark a full six steps to the opposite side of the cabin, where a smaller door led into dark and narrow passages. They vanished down one of them.

There was a moment of silence behind them. The king turned to Lady Valerie. "I take it he has something extremely important to discuss with her," he suggested mildly but with a twinkle in his warm brown eyes.

"Extremely," agreed Lady Valerie complacently. "I dare say they'll come tell us about it presently." She picked up a bit of embroidery, just as her husband came in through the door that James and Lark had gone out of. He was looking less like Prospero now, and more like an elderly Puck.

"My crew has ordered me off the decks," he said cheerfully. "No place for a landlubber, they tell me. Val, my love, I have just seen young James having a most fervent conversation with our granddaughter in the galley."

"Yes, I rather thought that's where he'd go," said Lady

Valerie. "I do hope the pots and pans are not falling about their heads," she added, as the small craft gave another violent lurch.

Sir Nicholas was not particularly interested in pots and pans. "It is my belief," he told his wife, "that James is proposing to Lark."

She nodded. "I should be extremely surprised if he were not."

Sir Nicholas looked pleased. "A fine boy," he remarked, sitting down on the nearest bit of bench. "But of course Lark must be much older before the matter can be considered seriously."

Lady Valerie's green eyes gleamed wickedly. "Jeremiah Talbot will be furious," she murmured with relish. "I shall write and tell him myself. As for Lark and James, there will be time and leisure—"

Something seemed to occur to her. She turned suddenly to the startled king. "In the meantime, Charles Stewart, I have a considerable number of things to say to you, and I don't suppose I shall ever have a better chance to say them, so you may as well make yourself comfortable."

About The Author

"As a child," Sally Watson says, "my nose was always in a book." Now the author of five books for young readers, among them *Mistress Malapert, Highland Rebel,* and *To Build a Land,* Miss Watson first began writing at the age of four, but soon discovered that "you can't always write the truth and be believed." This important realization came when she prepared a school composition on her experience of crashing full into a bear on his hind legs on Mount Rainier. No one ever believed this actually happened; so, Miss Watson claims, "I started making up stories that *were* believed."

Miss Watson received a B.A. in English from Reed College in Portland, Oregon. A proponent of Scottish dancing, handcrafts, cartoon sketches, Gilbert and Sullivan, and gardening, Miss Watson has traveled extensively in Europe and the Near East and lived for a year in England—providing herself with background material for LARK, which she wrote "because Lark wanted me to. She said it would be fun."